Ambushed
–in–
JaguarSwamp

Trailblazer Books

Also by Dave and Neta Jackson

Hero Tales: A Family Treasury of True Stories
From the Lives of Christian Heroes (Volumes I, II, & III)

Ambushed
–in–
JaguarSwamp

Dave & Neta Jackson

Story illustrations by
Julian Jackson

BETHANY HOUSE PUBLISHERS
MINNEAPOLIS, MINNESOTA 55438

Ambushed in Jaguar Swamp
Copyright © 1999
Dave and Neta Jackson

Illustrations © 1999
Bethany House Publishers

Story illustrations by Julian Jackson.
Cover design and illustration by Catherine Reishus McLaughlin.

Scripture quotations are from the King James Version of the Bible.

Published by Bethany House Publishers
A Ministry of Bethany Fellowship International
11400 Hampshire Avenue South
Minneapolis, Minnesota 55438
www.bethanyhouse.com

Printed in the United States of America by
Bethany Press International, Minneapolis, Minnesota 55438

Library of Congress Cataloging-in-Publication Data

Jackson, Dave.
    Ambushed in Jaguar Swamp / Neta & Dave Jackson.
        p.   cm. — (Trailblazer books)
    SUMMARY: Thirteen-year-old Kyemap wants to accept the
Christian teachings of Mr. Grubb, a missionary to the Lengua
Indians of Paraguay during the 1890s, but he fears the reaction of
the witch doctors.
    ISBN 0–7642–2014–4
    [1. Missionaries—Fiction. 2. Grubb, Barbrooke, 1865–1930—
Fiction. 3. Lengua Indians—Fiction. 4. Indians of South
America—Paraguay—Fiction. 5. Paraguay—Fiction.
6. Christian life—Fiction.] I. Jackson, Neta. II. Title.
III. Series.
PZ7.J132418 Am   1999
[Fic]—dc21   99–6490
                                                          CIP

Barbrooke Grubb first met Kyemap as a "young lad" in his native village of Yitlo-yimmaling, and it wasn't long before the boy went to live at the mission station to help Grubb. However, Kyemap was probably older than thirteen when this story took place.

The first reports to reach the mission station concerning the attack on Grubb said that he had been killed and named his attacker, and there soon developed a great deal of superstitious confusion about whether Grubb was dead or alive. We added the element of mystery for the sake of the story.

Though Kyemap went to Grubb's aid with Robert Graham and Sibeth, the second private trip is fictional.

Two events are chronologically out of order. Kyemap's baptism actually occurred in June 1899, and the showdown with the witch doctors took place in 1900, some three years after the main events of this story. It involved an attack on Kyemap's house and Grubb's response as described in this story but under more complicated circumstances.

The names of Richard Hunt's and Sibeth's wives are not known, so we have called them Mary and Hannah. We also shortened Kyemap's name from Kyemapsithyo, the mission station's name to Waik from Waikthlatingmangyalwa, and Poit's village to Namuk from Namukamyip. Grubb sometimes did the same in his writings, but have some fun trying to pronounce the longer names . . . at least once.

The "alligators" of the Chaco were probably caimans, a South American reptile similar to alligators and crocodiles that can exceed fifteen feet in length.

CONTENTS

DAVE AND NETA JACKSON are a full-time husband/wife writing team who have authored and coauthored many books on marriage and family, the church, relationships, and other subjects. Their books for children include the TRAILBLAZER series and *Hero Tales* volumes I, II, and III. The Jacksons have two married children, Julian and Rachel, and make their home in Evanston, Illinois.

Chapter 1

Sleeping with a Ghost

SPARKS SPRANG INTO THE VIOLET SKY, chased by flames that erupted when Kyemap dropped an armload of sticks on his small fire. He whirled around and stared toward the bushes that surrounded his small clearing. What had screamed? Was it the harmless paca rodent with its bloodcurdling cry . . . or was it a ghost?

Watching the dimly lit bushes for any sign of movement, the young boy carefully leaned down and drew a large stick from the fire. Small flames flickered from its other end. With two quick steps and a strong over-hand, Kyemap flung it toward the bushes, blue smoke looping behind. He did not care if the

bushes caught on fire. In fact, a small brush fire would end this frightening ordeal. The villagers would come running to put it out, and his test would be forgotten.

The stick landed with a rattle and a thud, and then some small animal scampered off through the dry leaves. Kyemap peered into the darkness a few moments longer—the scream must have come from a paca—and then he turned with a sigh and sat back down under the bottle trunk tree near the fire. He wrapped his blanket tighter around his shoulders and stared into the flickering flames.

This was a foolish test he had agreed to. Ever since the missionary Mr. Grubb had come to the Chaco, that vast wilderness plain of Paraguay, the witch doctors had been buzzing like cicadas in a tree on a hot night. At first they said the white man who told stories of Jesus was a fraud, and they would drive him away with their magic. But when their spells had no effect on him, they changed their tune and said that *he* was a witch doctor, too. "We witch doctors have special powers," Pinse-Tawa, the chief witch doctor warned. "The evil spirits don't hurt us because our powers are so strong. But the rest of you had better be careful. They can steal your soul and cause you to die."

But Mr. Grubb had only laughed. "They are just trying to frighten you," he said to the Indians in the Lengua langauge. "When you are afraid, they have power over you, and you will do what they tell you to do even though they are not chiefs.

Jesus will free you from that fear."

The debate had gone on and on as Mr. Grubb traveled around the Chaco visiting the different Lengua villages. On his third visit to Kyemap's village, Mr. Grubb had announced that he was building a mission station at Waik on the north bank of the river Negro. "Anyone who wants to come and learn about Jesus can live there," he said. "I will also teach you better ways to plant your crops and raise sheep and cattle."

Kyemap was tempted to laugh at the white missionary's terrible accent and use of the wrong Lengua words sometimes. But the rules Mr. Grubb made for anyone coming to live at the mission station were plain enough to understand.

1. No babies are to be killed.
2. No beer is to be brewed or drunk on the station.
3. Feasts are to continue no longer than three days.
4. People must work when asked to help.
5. No cattle are to be killed without Mr. Grubb's permission.

Kyemap had been one of the first people to settle in the village that quickly sprang up outside the mission station. "Go and discover the truth about this white man," Kyemap's father had said, "so that all our people may know." Soon almost two hundred came from far and wide to live in the village. Among them were Pinse-Tawa and two of his assistant witch doctors. "Every village needs a witch doctor or two or three," they said. But when they were reminded that they had claimed that Mr. Grubb was a witch doctor, they shrugged and said, "But he's a foreign witch doctor."

Foreign or not, Kyemap soon grew to like the tall white man with the bushy eyebrow on his lip. The Lengua people did not have beards, and when two or three hairs would occasionally sprout from a man's chin, he would quickly pluck them out. Grubb, however, had hair all over his face, far too much to pull it out, so he shaved it off every day with a sharp knife . . . except on his upper lip. There he let it grow like an extra eyebrow. All the Indians laughed when it wiggled as he talked.

In spite of the rules against killing babies at Waik, the witch doctors managed to kill some of them anyway to maintain the people's superstition. Whenever twins were born, the witch doctors said to kill them because one would be weak. And if the first child born to a couple was a girl, she would be killed because the witch doctors said she would bring bad luck. The same thing happened if a baby was born with unusually dark skin or if the father deserted the mother before the child's birth.

These practices brought much grief to the people, but the witch doctors controlled them. In fact, there were so many reasons for killing babies that the whole tribe was in danger of dying out. "This killing of your babies must stop!" Mr. Grubb shouted after the third child had been killed at Waik. "The witch doctors are telling you wrong!"

Just that afternoon Mr. Grubb had invited all the Lengua people who had been learning about Jesus to come to his house. Being only thirteen years old, Kyemap did not know if he was welcome, but he had been coming to Mr. Grubb's classes. So he stood at the back of a group of twenty or so Lengua people as they gathered before the verandah of Mr. Grubb's house. Pinse-Tawa came, too. He stood with his blanket wrapped tightly around his thin, crooked body. A deep frown etched his pock-marked face, and his uncombed hair was full of ashes.

Five other foreigners joined Mr. Grubb on his veranda. They were Richard Hunt, his wife, Mary, and Andrew Pride—English missionaries who had come to assist Grubb at the Waik station. To the side stood Sibeth, a German cart-maker, and his wife, Hannah, who had begun working for the mission the year before, in 1895. Sibeth built and drove the big-wheeled carts that carried supplies to the mission. Hannah was the daughter of a German colonist who had settled about sixty miles east along the Paraguay River near the town of Concepción.

After greeting everyone, Mr. Grubb asked in a confident voice, "What is the thing the Lengua people fear most?"

He looked around at the Indians until one said, "The bones of a dead horse?"

Grubb shook his head. "No, no. That won't do. Horse bones may be scary, but they're not that bad.

Why, one time I saw Chief Mechi walk right across the bones of a dead horse. What's more frightening than horse bones?"

"The darkness," offered another Indian.

"Ah yes, but why?" asked Grubb.

"Because the spirits of the dead roam the night," answered the Indian.

"And isn't the grave of a recently killed baby the most frightening place of all at night?" asked Grubb.

Kyemap nodded his head while other Indians murmured their agreement. Then, before Kyemap realized what was happening, Mr. Grubb pointed at him and said, "What do you say, Kyemap? Why is the grave of a baby the most frightening place of all?"

Kyemap shrank back until the man standing in front of him hid him from Grubb's view.

"Come on, now. Speak up," said Grubb as he moved to the side where he could see the boy. "I really want to know."

Finally, Kyemap mumbled, "It is because a baby is too small to know who killed it, and so its ghost will haunt anyone who comes near, especially at night."

"Is that right?" asked Grubb, looking right at Pinse-Tawa.

The old witch doctor nodded his head and looked down as he scuffed his feet in the dust. "It is very dangerous to go near a grave at night. I don't like to do it myself, and I am the most powerful witch doctor of the Lengua people."

"Good," said Grubb. He rubbed his hands together

as though he were warming them on a frosty morning. "Then if you think a baby's recent grave is the most scary place at night, I will prove it is powerless. Kyemap, you are only thirteen, the youngest person here this afternoon and therefore the least skilled in magic. I want you to do something for me, and I promise you that you will be completely safe."

Kyemap's knees almost folded when Grubb selected him. The "proof" Mr. Grubb wanted him to provide was to spend the night by the grave under the bottle trunk tree where the body of the murdered baby had been buried that very morning. If nothing happened to him during the night, then everyone would know that the witch doctors had lied.

That was how he had ended up alone out here in the dark with nothing but his blanket and a small fire to protect him.

The scream in the dark came again, this time from the other side of the clearing. Kyemap turned that way, his forehead wrinkled, his eyes wide to see into the night. Maybe it wasn't a paca after all. How could a little rodent get all the way from one side of the clearing to the other so quickly? He had heard something scamper off through the leaves when he threw the stick, but wouldn't a ghost pretend to be something else if it was trying to fool you . . . if it was trying to get close enough to grab your soul?

This was a terrible mistake!

"O great Creator of all things, Jesus, the God Mr. Grubb tells us about. If You exist, if You are good, if You care about me, please do not let the ghost of that

poor baby take my soul," whimpered Kyemap as he
stared at the edge of the clearing.

And then under the edge of the bushes, he saw

movement in the grass. He jumped to his feet and was almost ready to flee for the village when a paca sat up on its haunches and chattered at him through its buckteeth. Kyemap jumped toward it, waving his outstretched arms. The little creature screamed again, and ran off into the night.

"A paca. Just a paca, a silly paca!" he repeated to himself again and again as he paced back and forth beside his fire, not realizing that he was almost stepping on the new grave. "A ghost might make the sound of little feet in the leaves in order to fool me, but no ghost would take on the form of a paca." Then he slowed, "Or would it? A ghost is supposed to be hard to see. But if you could see it, would it look like the baby? Or . . . ? No, I'm sure I saw a paca!"

He walked back to the tree and sat down again. He stared at the little grave on the other side of the fire. Then he looked back toward the brush and frowned. On the other hand, in the dark one might mistake a baby for a large paca. It had looked like a paca because it sat up and chattered and ran off into the brush . . . but a ghost, could a ghost do that? How could he know?

Kyemap tried to calm his trembling body. He would not give in to panic. Mr. Grubb had warned him that he would have to resist fear. He had prayed, and that was just before he had actually seen the . . . the—could he believe it had been only a paca? Mr. Grubb had talked about faith, believing that God loved you and heard your prayers. Had God shown him the paca as an answer to his prayer?

"O God, I want to believe it was You who showed me the paca." The night was so long, and he was so tired. Kyemap closed his eyes and leaned forward, resting his head on his arms on his knees. "I want to believe it was You. I want to believe it was You." He kept whispering the prayer. . . .

The sky was turning pale yellow and his fire was nothing but glowing ashes when he awoke. He stood up and wrapped his blanket around him and looked around the clearing. He was alive after all! No ghost had attacked him. Though everything was still a shade of gray, he could see clearly. He had thrown the stick in the bushes over that direction. In the opposite direction he had seen the . . . yes, it must have been a paca.

He touched some dry grass to the coals and blew until a flame burst forth. Then he added twigs and sticks until the fire's cheery warmth calmed his shivering. He opened his blanket, stretched his arms with the blanket held by its corners so that he looked like a bat, and took a deep breath. When he wrapped it back around him, he walked slowly to the spot where he had seen the . . . He knelt down and examined the grass. There, like large black seeds, were eight shiny pellets. He crushed one between his thumb and first finger. It was soft and damp. A big grin spread across his face as he stood up.

✧ ✧ ✧ ✧

All the people gathered around that morning

when Kyemap marched back into the village. Children reached out to touch him, and the adults asked if he was all right. "Of course I am fine," he said confidently. "Mr. Grubb told you the witch doctors were wrong."

"But what happened?" they asked.

"I will tell you when Mr. Grubb has finished his breakfast," he said.

Mr. Grubb did not wait to finish his breakfast when Kyemap arrived at his house. Instead, he took his cup of tea and went outside where he rang the mission bell, inviting the whole village to gather and hear Kyemap's report. The witch doctors came sullenly; Pinse-Tawa was frowning darkly.

Kyemap told his story slowly, not leaving out any detail as he described the scream in the dark and the scurrying feet through the leaves. "Then there was another scream from the other side of the clearing," Kyemap said in a hushed voice. "I was so afraid that I prayed to the Creator God as Mr. Grubb told me to do. And then . . . and then, guess what happened?" He stopped and looked around. "A paca popped its head up out of the grass and chattered at me. That was right after I prayed.

"And, of course," he concluded, "you can all see that I have returned home safely. So Mr. Grubb must be right. There is nothing to fear." He glanced toward Pinse-Tawa.

The old witch doctor just closed his eyes and shook his head, but one of the younger witch doctors spoke up. "You are very foolish to mock the spirits," he warned. "They may have had mercy on you this once, but now *everyone* may be in danger. I think we should all leave this village."

"Why should we leave when I have proved there is nothing to fear," said Kyemap in a challenging voice.

Pinse-Tawa cleared his throat and said, "You speak too quickly. Ghosts can make noise in leaves that sound like an animal scampering away. They can even look like a paca."

"Yes, I thought of that," said Kyemap, "but can they eat?"

"Of course not." The witch doctor spat on the ground. "Everyone knows that."

"Is that so, Mr. Grubb?" asked Kyemap.

The missionary shrugged. "I don't even believe in ghosts, but . . . " Then he smiled. "After Jesus rose from the dead, His disciples thought He might be a ghost, so He ate some fish with them to demonstrate that He was alive. So I guess that proves ghosts—if they exist at all—can't eat."

Kyemap grinned broadly, stood taller, and tilted his chin toward the witch doctor. "Then I'll go sleep out there again tonight."

Pinse-Tawa shook his head. "You tempt the spirits, foolish boy. I rattled my gourd all night to make powerful magic to keep that ghost away from you, and now you mock me." Then his eyes got very big and he leaned toward Kyemap. "In the dark of the night, how can you be so sure that what you saw was a paca and not the ghost of the baby?"

"Because of these," Kyemap said as he held out his hand with the dark pellets in it for everyone to see. "If ghosts cannot eat, they cannot make droppings!"

Chapter 2

The Frog Talker

KYEMAP SLEPT OUT UNDER the bottle trunk tree the next night and was not even awakened by a paca. He was so tired after being scared the night before that he didn't wake up until the sun was high above the scrubby trees of the Chaco.

When he returned to the village, people nodded their heads knowingly and smiled at him with respect. But the witch doctors scowled. Kyemap did not understand the witch doctors' anger until he heard people repeating what he'd said. He was hoeing weeds in the pumpkin patch that afternoon. One woman stood up, drew her dirty hand across her sweaty forehead, and said to another, "Do you think it will finally rain tonight?" The other woman looked at the sky where only a few clouds had gathered and answered, "If ghosts cannot eat, they cannot make droppings." Then they both laughed.

Kyemap didn't understand what they meant. What did ghosts—or pacas—have to do with rain? But in the next few days, he heard the saying several times.

"Will One-Eye marry that White-Partridge girl now?" gossiped some girls gathering sticks for cooking fires. "If ghosts cannot eat, they cannot make droppings!" came the lighthearted answer.

A woman said admiringly, "Isn't Short-Blanket a good hunter?" Her husband snorted, "If ghosts cannot eat, they cannot make droppings."

The phrase had become a new saying among the people, meaning, "No way," "Not a chance," or "It'll never happen." Every time the people said it, they laughed and remembered how the witch doctors had been wrong.

Kyemap knew that was exactly what Mr. Grubb had hoped for. The power of the witch doctors had been reduced, and the people were less afraid. Maybe the baby killing would stop . . . at least at Waik. But Kyemap also knew the witch doctors would not quickly forget who had made them look like fools.

The young boy shrugged it off. He was enjoying the daily Bible classes Mr. Grubb taught to villagers who were interested. Even more important, Mr. Grubb had just invited him to be his personal assistant, working in his house so that he could learn more about God. "Each day I'll give you a Bible lesson, and when you are ready to follow Jesus, I will baptize you as a Christian," said Grubb.

✧ ✧ ✧ ✧

Mr. Grubb had been sick with the fever again. As Kyemap hurried to the missionary's house with some of Mrs. Hunt's good broth to build back Grubb's strength, he saw a familiar figure walking into Waik. "Oh no, not Poit," muttered Kyemap.

Poit was Kyemap's distant cousin. The young man lived on the western frontier of Lengua country near the borders with the Toothli and Suhin tribes. Poit was a small-time trader, traveling a good deal and often carrying news from one village to another.

"Well, if it isn't my little cousin from the swamp," Poit said when he saw Kyemap. "Take me to meet this white man I've been hearing so much about. How did you get to be his personal helper? I didn't realize you were old enough to start your own fire."

Kyemap grimaced and rolled his eyes. Of all his relatives, why did Poit have to show up? It seemed like he never missed a chance to try to make Kyemap look foolish. Kyemap was tempted to call him "Poit, Poit, Poit." After all, that was how he had gotten his name. His first words as a toddler had copied the croak of the little green tree frog: *"Poit, poit, poit."*

"I hear this foreigner is some kind of a witch doctor. How did you manage to work for him?" asked

Poit as they walked through the dusty village.

Not knowing whether his cousin would use his report as another way to make fun of him, Kyemap reluctantly told of his nighttime vigil under the bottle trunk tree.

But to his surprise, Poit did not laugh. "That wasn't my private hunting lodge, was it?" he said with a scowl. Poit had hollowed out a bottle trunk tree near the Sievo River where he sometimes stayed when hunting in the area. Once he had shown it to Kyemap.

"No, no. This tree is very close to the village," assured Kyemap. "You can see it from the sheep pens right over there."

"It better not have been my hunting lodge. You know what'll happen if you ever tell anyone. It's private!" he warned. Then after a moment, he dropped his angry tone and changed the subject. "I've never had much use for those witch doctors myself. They're always begging for food and never do any work. If this foreigner is more powerful, maybe it is good for you to become his friend, cousin. But Pinse-Tawa's not going to like it." Just then Poit looked up at the crooked figure approaching them from the side. "Speaking of the devil's own," he whispered, "look there."

Pinse-Tawa was walking toward them with a great limp—something the old witch doctor did on occasion, Kyemap thought, just to get people's attention and sympathy. "The people are so glad you have come!" Pinse-Tawa said, holding his left hand out toward Poit as he got closer.

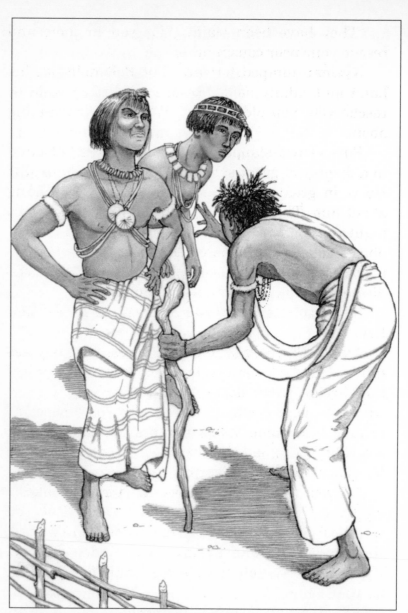

Poit stopped. With his hands on his hips and his head tipped to the side, he said flatly, "Why is that?"

"They have been waiting for you to come and rescue your poor cousin here."

Kyemap jumped forward, but Poit held out his hand and calmly said, "Rescue my little cousin or rescue you, you old fleabag? What are you talking about?"

Pinse-Tawa slapped his head with his left hand in a display of great surprise. "Have you not heard? He is in great danger. All the people are talking about him. The missionary forced him to spend two nights out on the Chaco alone—" he paused for emphasis and then whispered as though he were sharing a secret—"near the new grave of a poor baby who died under, uh, unfortunate circumstances."

"Unfortunate circumstances? I can imagine," said Poit.

"Well!" Pinse-Tawa rolled his eyes. "The boy has lost his mind. He came completely under the spell of this foreign witch doctor, and we can't do a thing with him. That is why we are so glad you have come to take him home to his parents. How they must grieve! I feel so bad that we couldn't help, but these foreigners are very powerful."

"If you weren't as sneaky as a rattlesnake, I might pay attention to you," Poit said. "But you won't poison me with your crazy schemes. I'll meet this man and make up my own mind. Come on, Kyemap. Don't you have some broth for this Mr. Grubb?"

Kyemap glanced out of the corner of his eye at his older cousin. Poit had always been a schemer and certainly not his favorite relative, but he didn't appear to be under the power of the witch doctors. Maybe it was good that he had come.

Grubb was slouched on the veranda of his house, still weak from the fever. But as soon as Kyemap introduced Poit and said that he came from a village on the western frontier, Mr. Grubb perked up. "I've always wanted to make contact with the Toothli and Suhin tribes. Could you help me, Poit?"

All afternoon Poit and Mr. Grubb talked about the distant tribes. Finally, as the cousins were leaving, Grubb said, "There are legends that tribes of giants and pigmies are living in the forests to the west. Do you know about this?"

Poit laughed. "No. Those were just stories to scare the Spaniards away. Do you know that they never succeeded in exploring the Chaco? Even with all their guns, we always chased them away before they got very far."

That night as Kyemap and Poit sat by the fire outside Kyemap's hut, Pinse-Tawa and two other witch doctors came and sat near them. Kyemap wanted to get up and walk away; given the sour look on Poit's face, he figured his cousin felt the same way. Only politeness prevented them. "Why are you interested in this foreigner?" challenged the youngest witch doctor.

Poit ate a pumpkin seed and spit out the hulls. He ate another and another, spitting the hulls into the fire before he answered. "Two moons ago," he said without looking at the witch doctor, "I met a very old wise man in the West who was dying. He told me a prophecy that has been passed down from generation to generation among our people. Possibly you know of it since you are so smart," he said sarcastically, "but I had not heard it before." Poit stopped and put another seed into his mouth. Slowly he cracked the hull, spit it into the fire, and chewed the meat.

"How should we know whether we have heard the prophecy if you don't tell us what it is," said the young witch doctor impatiently.

Kyemap noticed a twinkle in Poit's eye as he teased the witch doctors. "I thought your magic might be powerful enough to know what I was thinking without me saying anything," he mocked.

Pinse-Tawa snorted and looked away.

"No?" said Poit. "Well, the prophecy said that someday foreigners will come to our land who will reveal the mysteries of the spirit world, and they will help our people. But it also included a warning: If we reject the message of the foreigners, we will cease to exist. Have you heard of that prophecy?"

The two younger witch doctors shrugged and looked at each other. "Who can tell what some wrinkled old goat might say? Why should we pay attention?" They did not look at Pinse-Tawa, who was about as wrinkled and old as a person could be.

Pinse-Tawa frowned at their disrespect. "Well, I have heard of that prophecy," he growled, "but foreigners have tried to enter our land since the time of my grandfather. They came only to steal and kill."

"That is true," admitted Poit. "The foreigners have cheated and robbed us, and they brought men with guns who sometimes killed our people. But this Mr. Grubb—is he not different? I have heard that he has traveled in the Chaco for five years now, and he has never killed anyone. I have heard that he and the missionaries with him do not cheat or rob. I have heard that he does not hide behind armed soldiers when he travels. I have heard that he sometimes travels completely alone in the wilderness. Is that not true?"

"You have heard a lot," said Pinse-Tawa scornfully. "But I think he is here to steal our way of life."

Kyemap spoke up. "The only thing he will 'steal,' as you put it, is your power to frighten and control the people."

Pinse-Tawa shrugged, and everyone sat silently until the fire needed another stick.

Kyemap got up and put on some more wood, but he remained standing. He had listened long enough to not be rude. Even though he was the youngest person present, it was his hut and his fire and therefore his right to signal when the conversation was over. Slowly, the witch doctors rose and nodded their good-byes. As they were leaving, Kyemap said quietly, "What if the old prophecy is true, and Grubb and his assistants *are* the foreigners who bring the *Tasik Amyaa* [Good News]? What will happen if we reject it?"

✧ ✧ ✧ ✧

Days passed, but Poit did not build a hut of his own. "Why build a hut when I can sleep in yours?" he said to Kyemap. "Besides, I have more important things to do. I am talking business with Mr. Grubb. He's going to give me a herd of cattle, and I'll become very rich. You'll see." Indeed, by the time Kyemap got to Mr. Grubb's house each morning, Poit and Mr. Grubb were so busy talking that there was no time for Kyemap's Bible lesson. Kyemap did his work in the house, then went out to the garden to harvest melons or sweet potatoes or manioc root. Sometimes he repaired the pen for the sheep.

Traditionally, the Lengua people allowed their sheep and goats to roam freely, and wolves or even a jaguar often killed them. Mr. Grubb said that such helpless animals should be kept in pens near the village, but Kyemap thought it was a lot of work repairing the fences. He stood up from weaving new sticks into the animal pen. It was so much hotter out in the sun than it was back on Mr. Grubb's veranda with a cool glass of tea.

He wiped his brow and looked toward the mission station. Why was Mr. Grubb spending all his time with Poit and none with him? He was the one who braved the ghost under the bottle trunk tree at night! He was the one who helped Grubb reduce the power of the witch doctors! What happened to his Bible lessons?

He swung around to go get more sticks and bumped into one of the witch doctors who was walking past. "Watch where you are going," snapped

Kyemap, still feeling upset. "You've got the whole Chaco to walk on, so why do you need to walk down this fence as though it were a narrow trail in the forest?"

The witch doctor ducked his head and raised a hand like he was warding off a blow and hurried on without saying a word. "Wait!" Kyemap called after him. "You've walked past here several times today. What are you doing? You lazy dogs never leave the shade of your palm tree unless you have some purpose. So why are you bothering me?"

But the witch doctor hurried on. Then Kyemap noticed Pinse-Tawa standing at the other end of the fence smoking a pipe. Kyemap looked around. It was very strange for anyone to smoke a pipe alone without sharing it with others. Why was he standing out here by the animal pen as though he enjoyed the scenery?

The sticks Kyemap needed were in a pile beyond Pinse-Tawa, so he headed for them. "Good day, Old One," he said as he approached the witch doctor.

Pinse-Tawa grunted. But as he passed, Kyemap noticed a quick movement out of the corner of his eye. He turned in time to see the witch doctor step away from the fence and plant his misshapen bare foot right where Kyemap had walked.

Kyemap flinched, thinking the old man intended to hit him, but he didn't raise his hand. Then Kyemap saw what he was doing. He was stepping on Kyemap's shadow. The witch doctors were working magic on him.

Chapter 3

The Magic Show

MR. GRUBB SHOOK HIS HEAD in bewilderment. "I don't understand," he said in Lengua. "So what if he steps on your shadow? What harm can that do?"

"It's magic," said Kyemap. "They are trying to kill me!"

Grubb threw up his hands. "How can stepping on your shadow possibly hurt you?"

Kyemap shrugged, but his wide eyes still revealed his fear.

"Look," said the missionary. "If we were going on a journey, walking side by side, I would be stepping on your shadow and you would be stepping on mine all day long. What

33

difference would it make?"

"Yes, but we wouldn't be using any magic on each other," said Kyemap.

"Exactly, because there is no power in their foolish spells and superstitions. Didn't you prove that yourself the nights you spent under the bottle trunk tree?"

Kyemap stood looking down at the floor.

Finally, Grubb said, "Alright, alright, so you are afraid. Let's approach this another way. Why do you think they might be wanting to kill you?"

Kyemap shrugged.

"Poit," Mr. Grubb said, "do you have any idea why these witch doctors are upset with this boy?"

"They probably want to get rid of him. They've tried every day since I got here to get me to send him home, but so far"—Poit flipped his hand out, palm up, in a careless gesture—"they can't pay enough."

"Pay?" said Grubb. "You would accept a bribe to send your own cousin home?"

"Why not?" laughed Poit. "I'm learning business. But as my little cousin says, 'If ghosts cannot eat, they cannot make droppings.' Witch doctors have no money, so I don't send him home. That's why they have turned to magic."

"Well, how do we get them to leave him alone?" said Mr. Grubb.

"Use greater magic," offered Poit.

"Magic?" Grubb shook his head. "After all the time we've talked, do you think I came here to practice magic?"

"How should I know?" Poit retorted.

❖ ❖ ❖

That night the witch doctors said that they wanted all the people to meet in the small field between the village and the mission buildings. They had something very important to say to the people.

Mr. Grubb did not ring the mission bell to announce this meeting, but he and his assistant, Andrew Pride, came nevertheless and stood with the villagers.

After everyone had gathered before a large bonfire, Pinse-Tawa stood up and said, "The spirits have shown us that Kyemap must leave this place. He has been away from his home village for too long, and his spirit is in danger of getting lost."

Mr. Grubb stepped forward. "That is a lie. What has happened is that he has weakened your power, and to get it back, you want people to forget about him," he said.

"No," said Pinse-Tawa in a solemn voice. "It is the will of the spirits, not us."

"Spirits?" challenged Grubb. "You do not speak for spirits. Where is your authority?"

"You challenge my authority?" roared Pinse-Tawa in a voice that surprised everyone. "You watch this!"

At that moment he threw off his blanket and began dancing around the bonfire, shaking his rattle violently. All the villagers shrank back as his dancing got wilder and wilder, and then he stopped and faced the open Chaco in the direction where no one sat.

He leaned far forward, pursing his lips, and then spat something out into the knee-high grass.

"Is there a small child who saw where that seed landed?" he asked.

Three little hands shot up, and he picked a girl about four years old. "Go see what you find there," he said.

The girl looked at her mother and then ran into the grass, almost to the edge of the firelight. "A pumpkin," she squealed with delight, as she picked up one about the size of her head and brought it back.

The old witch doctor spat out three more seeds, and other children found a pumpkin where each landed. "Oos" and "ahs" from the villagers showed they were impressed.

"Stop," said Grubb. "Don't anyone move!" Then he walked over to one of the assistant witch doctors and pulled off his blanket. Two more pumpkins fell to the ground. Grubb also walked out into the grass and found three more pumpkins in the dark.

Coming back to the fire, he challenged, "When Pinse-Tawa was dancing around so wildly that you were watching his every move, these other fakers walked out in the grass and dropped the pumpkins for the children to find. It's a nice trick, but that's all it is. Seeds do not turn into pumpkins unless you plant them and wait a few weeks."

The villagers clapped their hands. "If ghosts cannot eat, they cannot make droppings," shouted one of the villagers from the back of the group. Everyone laughed, and Kyemap breathed a sigh of relief. He had not seen the assistant witch doctors hide the pumpkins in the grass, and until Grubb revealed their trick, it had looked like magic to him.

"You'll have to do better than that," said Grubb as he went to take his seat with the other villagers.

An angry scowl contorted Pinse-Tawa's face. "You want big magic? I will show you big magic!" Then he slowly walked to the other side of the fire and sat down with his back to the fire and all the people. Beside him stood his two assistants. For several minutes he sat there chanting. Then he spun around, creating a little cloud of dust. But he still sat on the other side of the fire from the crowd of villagers.

"Come here," he ordered, pointing to the little girl who had found the first pumpkin. Shyly, with her thumb in her mouth, the girl walked around the fire to the old man. He had her lie down in front of him as he continued his chanting and waved his hands above her body. Then he grabbed her bare stomach so that she cried out and sat halfway up. "Lie down," he shouted at her, and suddenly in his grimy hands there was a small kitten, meowing loudly and waving its paws with claws extended.

The witch doctor dropped the kitten on the ground, and it scampered away into the night. Then he grabbed the girl's stomach again. It was hard to see exactly what was happening through the smoke and flames, but suddenly he lifted up another kitten.

He tossed it aside, and it, too, ran off.

This he repeated a third time, and then he slowly stood up and stepped back beside his assistants. The girl lay on the ground whimpering for a few minutes, then got up and ran to her mother.

Everyone sat in stunned silence.

Kyemap stole a glance to see what Mr. Grubb was doing. He was just staring at the ground. But finally he stood up and said, "Well, I can't top that, and I can't explain it, but I assure you all that it was just a trick. I've learned some tricks in my day, too. Now, I'm not a witch doctor as some of you may think, and what I'm going to show you will prove it takes no special power to perform a good trick."

He stepped out in front of the people but not behind the bonfire. Then he whistled to call a dog over to him. The dog came, cautiously sniffing, and Grubb held up a small piece of paper for everyone to see. When he offered it to the dog, the dog quickly ate it, licking its nose and thrusting its head forward slightly as it swallowed the paper.

"Now," said Grubb, "watch very closely." He grabbed the dog's tail and pulled the paper from the tip of the tail. "You like that?" he said, holding the paper up for everyone to see.

They all clapped—all except the witch doctors— and Grubb did the trick again.

"Does anybody know how I did it?" he asked.

Everyone shook their heads.

"Kyemap, come here," he said. Then speaking to the villagers he added, "Any one of you could do this same trick, and I'll show you how.

"I put some chicken fat on the paper, which is what made the dog eat it. Here, Kyemap. Here's some paper and a little bit of fat. You try it, but make sure everyone can see what you are doing."

There was nothing unusual about a dog swallowing a small piece of paper with some tasty fat on it,

and the dog proved it in one gulp.

"In my other hand," said Grubb, "I had hidden a second small piece of paper that looked very much like the first piece of paper. It was easy to fold up so no one noticed it. A few moments later, when I was holding the dog's tail, I unfolded the paper and made it appear as though it came from the tip of the dog's tail. Here, Kyemap, you try it." He handed the paper to Kyemap, then said, "Show the people how the paper is hidden in your hand. Now grab the dog's tail and unfold the paper."

Everything worked just as he said, and soon everyone was clapping and cheering.

"Yes, that was fun, wasn't it? But it was just a trick. Let's all go home and get a good night's sleep."

As the people departed, the children chased the village dogs to see if they could do the trick, too. The witch doctors, however, walked off alone into the dark.

❖ ❖ ❖ ❖

In the middle of the night, Kyemap was awakened by a terrible commotion. People were running around and yelling. Something crashed into the back of his hut, and suddenly portions of the roof began flying off.

Kyemap jumped up and tripped over his water gourd as he tried to scramble out to see what was happening. Dogs were barking, and by the time he got outside, people were running past his hut yelling that they had seen a ghost.

He grabbed a small bundle of straw and held the end of it against the dimly burning coals of his fire. He blew on it until it ignited into a torch. Kyemap examined the backside of his hut, and sure enough, whole sections of the roof had been flipped off and lay several feet away on the ground.

"What's happening out there?" came the voice of Poit from inside.

"I don't know," said Kyemap.

By the time Poit joined him, several other villagers had torches and were surveying the damage. "It must have attacked the sheep," said a man standing at the edge of the village, peering off into the darkness. "I can see where they broke out of their pen. It looks like most of them ran off into the night. But I'm sure not going out there to try to find them in the dark."

"I know that I saw a ghost," said a frightened woman between sobs. "It was floating around above the roof of your hut, Kyemap. I think you've made the spirits angry."

Soon everyone was examining the torn-up roof of Kyemap's hut and shaking their heads. Some backed away from him as though he were the ghost.

"Now maybe you won't mock the spirits anymore," said one of the young witch doctors.

"Now maybe you'll go home to your own village," said the other. But Pinse-Tawa was nowhere to be seen.

No one slept the rest of that night, and by the

next morning, Kyemap had decided to return to his home village. He gathered his few belongings together into a small bundle. He looked over toward Mr. Grubb's house and shook his head. "I suppose I should at least tell him that I am leaving," he said as he walked slowly from the village to the mission station.

He expected the missionary to be angry with him as he explained what had happened during the night and his decision to leave. But instead, all Mr. Grubb said was, "I have had a little touch of the fever again, so I haven't gone out this morning. Would you please find Pinse-Tawa and bring him here to my house? I want to talk to him, and I want you to hear what I have to say."

Kyemap shrugged. If Mr. Grubb was sick, then obviously he had to help him. He went looking for Pinse-Tawa and found the old man outside the village sitting under the bottle trunk tree near the baby's grave. No one knew for certain, but it was probably Pinse-Tawa who had killed the baby. Parents seldom did the deed themselves. When the witch doctor said it had to happen, the new parents usually paid the witch doctor to do the killing.

As he approached the old man, Kyemap said, "I see you are not afraid of the baby's ghost."

Pinse-Tawa looked up in surprise. "No, no. I have charms that protect me . . . at least during the day." Then he changed the subject. "Will you be leaving Waik?"

"I plan to leave today," admitted Kyemap, looking at the ground. "But first Mr. Grubb wants to talk to you. He waits at his house. Will you come?"

The witch doctor got up and followed in silence.

Back at the mission station, Mr. Grubb met them on the veranda and said, "Come in, both of you. I want you to see something." He led them through the general room and out onto the dining and sleeping veranda that extended across the whole back of the house. It had a wall halfway up and screens above that on all three sides.

Grubb casually walked over to his bed and then removed one of the screens so as to create an open window facing the Lengua village. "I understand," said Grubb to Pinse-Tawa, "that there was a great disturbance in the village last night."

"Yes," said the witch doctor. "Many ghosts."

"And a few devils, no doubt," said Grubb. "Well, we can't let the village be disturbed like that again, can we?"

"No. They attacked this poor boy's hut. I think they are angry with him," said Pinse-Tawa.

Grubb grinned so that his mustache spread out flat under his nose. "I have a plan that should put an end to it. See my rifle here? If tonight—or any other night—those ghosts bother his hut, I'll just fire a few shots over there and scare them off. You think that will work?"

Pinse-Tawa's eyes got very large, and he began shaking. Finally, he muttered, "I don't think they will bother him anymore."

"Good," said Grubb. Then he turned to Kyemap.

"Then I don't see any reason why you need to leave. Our great witch doctor here is quite certain that you won't be bothered again. Is that good enough for you?"

Chapter 4

Alligator Stew

WHEN HE HAD FINISHED THE WORK in Mr. Grubb's house the next day, Kyemap decided he would just stay there unless Mr. Grubb told him to go out to the garden. He went out onto the veranda, where Poit and Mr. Grubb were talking.

"Let's go tomorrow," Poit was saying to Grubb when Kyemap sat down. "You want to take cattle to the Suhin and Toothli people as gifts? We can take the cattle as far as Namuk; I know of a good pasture for them not far from my village. Then I will take you to the Suhin and the Toothli people."

"I'm afraid I can't," said Grubb reluctantly. "In ten days, I have to go away, far away across the big water to my country of England. I have not had a furlough, a—" he fumbled for the right word, "—a vacation . . . Oh, you wouldn't understand that, either. Anyway, I have to go away. There is not enough time between now and then to visit the Suhin and the Toothli."

"That doesn't matter," said Poit. "I will be glad to look after the cattle for you at Namuk while you are gone. Then when you come back, you could make Namuk your base camp and visit the Suhin and Toothli."

Kyemap frowned. It wasn't like Poit to offer to look after livestock. His cousin liked to be free to travel whenever he felt like it.

But Mr. Grubb seemed to like the idea. "Well," he said, rubbing his chin thoughtfully, "we would have to take an oxcart with supplies and things to trade, and we'd have to build a house to store the supplies in until I come back." He brightened. "Yes, maybe that would work. I could drive the cart if you would help with herding the cattle."

"Of course," said Poit. "We could take my little cousin here. He ought to be good for herding cattle, and that would get him out of the way of these foolish witch doctors."

Kyemap looked away toward the Chaco, where a dust devil spun its way across the dry ground. He felt like a dust devil was spinning in his stomach the way his cousin always treated him like something extra that needed a reason to exist.

❖ ❖ ❖ ❖

Early the next morning, Sibeth, the German cart-maker, had two oxen hitched to a large-wheeled cart that he had loaded with all the items Mr. Grubb had ordered. With a small herd of seventeen cattle, Mr. Grubb, Poit, and Kyemap set out. Travel proved much slower than they expected. The early days of March 1896 seemed to evaporate as they cut a trail through scrub brush, forests, and swamp.

When they finally arrived at the Sievo River not far from the village of Paisiam—about fifteen miles south of Waik—Mr. Grubb pulled the oxcart to a stop along the edge of the steep riverbank some six feet above the water. He looked back toward Kyemap and Poit, who were following with the cattle, and yelled, "We're never going to make it to Namuk in time. I think we'd better build some kind of a storage hut in Paisiam. Chief Mechi is a good man. He will look out for our supplies and prevent anyone from taking them."

"But what about the cattle?" called Poit.

"Well, I suppose . . ." said Grubb, but the ox clos-est to the riverbank was pawing the soft ground so hard that the loud *thud, thud, thud* made it hard to talk. Grubb got down and walked back toward Kyemap and Poit. "I suppose you could take them on to Namuk, but are you sure you have a good pasture there? You can't turn cows out into a swampy area or they'll get disease, but they must have access to water at all times." Poit was nodding his head ea-gerly as Grubb spoke. "You've seen the pasture near Waik. Do you have something like that at Namuk?"

The ox that had been pawing the ground had loosened the dirt enough to kick it up onto its flanks in an attempt to drive off the tormenting horseflies. It kept pawing and kicking.

"Oh yes, much better," said Poit. "Namuk is built on a little hill with a lake all around. It is beautiful, and there is always water and good grass. Our goats and sheep do very well there."

"Sheep? But if too many sheep graze a pasture, it's no good for cattle," worried Grubb. "They eat the grass too short."

"No, no," said Poit. "Our grass grows tall." And he demonstrated with his hands a height of six or seven inches.

Suddenly, a commotion from the cart caused the three travelers to turn that way just in time to see the edge of the bank give way and the ox that had been pawing the ground slip over the edge, bellowing in horror as it scrambled to stop itself.

Terrified, the other ox pulled away from the crumbling edge with all its might; because the two were joined by the strong yoke, this was just the help the fallen ox needed to finally crawl back up the bank. Snorting and lunging with its eyes wide, the beast finally made it up onto flat ground, but its effort broke off more huge wedges of dirt. The last piece of the bank to cave in extended under the front wheel of the cart.

Kyemap, Poit, and Mr. Grubb ran toward the slowly toppling cart and grabbed its near side. Together with the oxen, they kept it from tipping into the river. But in the course of the tussle, the tongue of the cart broke. The loud splintering of the wood frightened the oxen even more.

"Steady those oxen!" yelled Mr. Grubb as the cart teetered on the brink. "Don't let them run away!"

Kyemap grabbed the reins and pulled with all his might to stop the frightened animals. The commotion, however, had startled the cattle, and they bolted away through the brush in several directions, their tails high and their hooves kicking behind them.

Poit and Grubb were barely keeping the cart from going over the bank. Once Kyemap had the oxen under control, Mr. Grubb grunted, "Now, wrap those reins around that stump and carefully get the rope out of the back of this cart."

Kyemap quickly tied up the oxen and then rummaged in the cart, taking care not to do anything that would push it over the edge. Once he had the rope, he tied it securely to the cart and then to the oxen's yoke. "Good, good," said Grubb. "Now slowly urge the oxen forward—we can't hold this thing much longer!"

Indeed, Mr. Grubb and Poit were straining their muscles so hard that their arms shook, and sweat dripped freely from their faces. The oxen, which were still frightened, refused to pull together. When one pulled, the other thought that it was being pushed toward the river. As soon as Kyemap got that one settled, the other shied away.

"Forget the reins!" yelled Mr. Grubb. "Grab their nose rings! They've got to know you are in control and that you are not trying to pull them toward the river."

Kyemap did as Grubb said, and sure enough, the oxen calmed down and finally pulled together. The rope tightened until it vibrated like the wings of a hummingbird. If it broke, Kyemap knew the ends might whip around and injure someone. But slowly, their huge muscles straining, the oxen managed to pull the cart up onto level ground and away from the crumbling bank. Poit and Grubb fell panting to the ground.

When they'd caught their breath, the cousins started the task of rounding up the scattered cattle. An hour later, Mr. Grubb called to Kyemap and Poit from the river. He was standing up in a dugout canoe waving to them. "I borrowed this canoe from Chief Mechi!" he yelled. "I'm going to go across the river to that grove and find a nice straight sapling I can cut down to make a new tongue for the cart. I'll be back soon."

As Grubb paddled across the river, Kyemap sat down on the bank where the sparse shade of a tree fell, but Poit walked away from the river's edge and crawled into the shade under the cart to escape the heat of the afternoon sun.

✧ ✧ ✧ ✧

Kyemap did not know how long he had dozed when the sound of the wooden canoe awoke him as it scraped ashore on the grassy sandbar that hooked out into the river a short distance downriver. He saw Grubb stand up and, using his paddle like a cane to steady him-

self, walk toward the front of the tipsy canoe. Suddenly, what had looked like an old brown log half-buried in the grass rose up and charged Grubb.

"Alligator!" screamed Kyemap in warning, but Grubb had already seen the reptile and was jamming his paddle into its gaping mouth. The huge monster crunched the paddle into matchsticks and kept hissing at Grubb, taking a step closer each moment.

"Poit, come quickly!" yelled Kyemap to his cousin, who was already running toward the riverbank. "We've got to help him!" he said, pointing toward Grubb.

But instead of hurrying downstream to where the gentle slope out onto the sandbar would make it easy to run to Grubb's aid, Poit stood riveted, watching the struggle, his hand outstretched toward Kyemap as if to stop him.

Kyemap couldn't understand why his cousin hesitated, but by the time he looked back at Mr. Grubb, the missionary had picked up the pole he had cut to make a new cart tongue and rammed its pointed tip down the alligator's throat. Then he began hammering on the other end with his ax to drive it deeper. The alligator roared like a sick cow and began flipping its tail around to break free, but Grubb kept on hammering the pole until he drove it into the monster's vital organs, and the creature ceased to fight.

Kyemap's mouth dropped open. "Can you believe that?"

But behind him, his cousin had not moved an inch. Poit was staring at the missionary as though he had seen a vision. "Poit!" snapped Kyemap. "What's the matter with you? Why didn't you go help Mr. Grubb?"

Poit muttered something under his breath, but Kyemap caught the words: "They might find a man's bones out here in the Chaco, but who could prove how he died?" Then, abruptly, he began walking along the bank and turned down onto the sandbar.

"What do you mean, Poit?" demanded Kyemap, running to catch up. "Why didn't you go help him?"

"Forget it," Poit said with a wave of his hand. "It doesn't matter now; he killed the dragon alone. We will help repair the cart."

❖ ❖ ❖ ❖

The red sun was falling into the shimmering edge of the Chaco as Grubb climbed onto the cart and urged the oxen toward the village of Paisiam. Kyemap and Poit came along behind, driving the cattle they'd rounded up from the surrounding brush. Across the top of the cart was tied the huge body of the alligator, the largest Kyemap had ever seen. "It will make a good gift to Chief Mechi for having left his canoe down here," said Grubb.

"And for breaking his paddle," added Kyemap. They all laughed.

Late that night in the village of Paisiam, everyone feasted on alligator stew.

❖ ❖ ❖ ❖

The next morning, after several villagers had helped build a storage hut and Chief Mechi had promised to care for Mr. Grubb's supplies, the missionary turned to Poit. "Take good care of these cattle for me," he said. "But remember, they are not your cattle. They belong to me. You are just their caretaker until I get back. Then we will use them to benefit your people and to contact the Suhin and the Toothli people."

Poit nodded but did not answer or look at Mr. Grubb. "Poit!" Mr. Grubb said sharply. "Are you listening to me? You are not to kill any of them. They belong to me."

Still, Poit did not look at him. "What's the matter?" asked Mr. Grubb. "Are you upset that I'm taking Kyemap back to Waik? You said you could find someone else to help you herd the cattle on to Namuk. What is it—another sixty miles?"

Finally, Poit answered. "Yes, yes, that's fine. You can take him. I will take the cattle." But he still refused to look Mr. Grubb in the eye.

Chapter 5

Thirteen Moons of Waiting

KYEMAP FELT LIKE AN ANT clinging to a witch doctor's rattle as he tried to stay on the seat of the empty oxcart as it bounced over the dry Chaco on its way back to Waik. To keep their insides from turning to jelly, he and Mr. Grubb took turns walking beside the cart until they came to a marshy area where the softer ground cushioned their ride.

"You've been helping me for quite a while now," said Mr. Grubb when Kyemap climbed back up on the cart beside him. "What have you learned?"

Kyemap looked at the missionary as they rolled along.

Was this some kind of a test? How could he list everything he had learned over the past few months! And what if he forgot to mention the most important lessons? Finally, he said, "I have learned much, and I thank you for letting me work in your house. I've even been learning English: *Good morning. Good evening. Would you like some tea?*"

"Good, good. But what have you learned from the Bible? Have you decided to follow Jesus with your life?" asked the missionary.

Kyemap watched the rolling muscles under the hide of the oxen as they plodded step by step—one, two, one, two. They had taken twenty steps since Mr. Grubb had asked his question, and Kyemap knew he had better answer pretty soon. One, two, one, two, one two . . . He had learned a lot about Jesus, but what could he say? Making such a decision would make him the first Lengua to convert to the Christian faith. He didn't much care what the witch doctors thought. He had become convinced that they were powerless compared to Mr. Grubb's God. But would God really care for a young Lengua boy, or would Kyemap be left alone without even the traditions of his people?

"Do you pray like I taught you?" asked Grubb.

"Sometimes," mumbled Kyemap.

"Good," said the missionary. "You keep asking God to show himself true to you."

After a few moments Grubb continued. "I will be gone for thirteen months—thirteen moons—but I will return. Maybe when I get back you will be ready for baptism."

❖ ❖ ❖ ❖

Mr. Grubb left for his trip on March 24, 1896. The date meant nothing to Kyemap, and he had no idea where England was. All Mr. Grubb could tell him was that it was far down the river Negro and far down the river Paraguay (which Kyemap had never seen, but had heard about) and far across the big salt sea where summer was winter, and winter was summer.

Sometimes on the Chaco, shallow saltwater ponds collected after a long rain. When the hot sun dried up the water and baked the mud until it was hard and cracked, the Lengua people scraped white crystals off the top. It was good for preserving meat. But Kyemap knew nothing of a salt sea or big canoes that, like thistledown, caught the wind and sailed away.

The work of the mission station was carried on by the other missionaries: Richard and Mary Hunt, and Andrew Pride. Gardens were planted, sheep tended, cattle fed, and the missionaries taught Bible classes. Kyemap attended and listened quietly for one moon and then two and then three, but finally he lost interest. Mr. Grubb had said he would return in thirteen moons, but that was nearly forever.

Then one very hot and dry evening Poit returned to Waik. "Where is Mr. Grubb?" he asked Kyemap as he sat down beside the boy's fire. "I must warn that foreigner."

"Warn him of what?" asked Kyemap.

Poit looked around to make sure no one else was listening. "I have had a dream," he said in a whisper. "In it Mr. Grubb drowned. I must warn him."

"He is not here," said Kyemap. "He told you that he would not return for thirteen moons, and so far only six moons have passed. Besides, it hasn't rained in so long, there isn't a puddle deep enough for drowning."

"Nevertheless," said Poit with a shrug, "if I cannot warn him, he will surely die."

Kyemap eyed his cousin closely. When the alligator had almost killed Mr. Grubb near Paisiam, Poit had hesitated to go to his aid. Now Poit was again acting like he didn't care whether Mr. Grubb lived or died, so why had he come so far to warn Mr. Grubb? Finally, Kyemap asked, "Was the water in which Mr.

Grubb drowned salty or sweet?"

"How should I know?" said Poit. "Do you think I tasted it in my dream?"

"I only asked because he is traveling on salty water. If the water in which he drowned in your dream was not salty, then it was a false dream," Kyemap reasoned. "Besides, Mr. Grubb does not believe in dreams."

Poit snorted in disgust. "How can one not believe in dreams? They tell everything." He tossed a few sticks on the fire and then stared into the flames for a long time without blinking. Finally, he declared, "He is dead. He will never return. These missionaries are not the fulfillment of the ancient prophecy. I will go home and have a feast with his cattle because now they are mine."

"But you can't!" said Kyemap as his cousin stood up. He, too, got to his feet. "You promised to care for his cattle, and thirteen moons have not yet passed."

Kyemap had grown almost as tall as his cousin and stood looking him in the eye. "They are not your cattle!" he said boldly.

"He is dead!" declared Poit. "The cattle belong to me."

Kyemap argued some more, but nothing he said made any difference to Poit. Later, when they had wrapped their blankets around themselves and Poit was snoring softly, Kyemap watched his cousin in the flickering light from his fire. Why did he care what Poit did? Was he afraid that Mr. Grubb would return and be upset with Poit? Or was he afraid that the Lengua superstitions might be true and Mr. Grubb would never return?

Probably a little of both. He wrestled with both questions a long time before he fell asleep.

The next morning, through half-closed eyes, Kyemap watched as Poit got up and roasted a sweet potato in the coals of the fire. After Poit had turned it several times, he stabbed it with a stick and pulled it from the fire. "Well, I'm returning to Namuk," he announced as Kyemap sat up and rubbed his eyes.

Poit wrapped his blanket around himself with a flourish. "I am going to throw a great feast," he said. "Who knows how long it will last? It may go on forever, and the grateful people may make me chief. At least your Mr. Grubb has done something good for me." Poit started to walk away, but then he turned back to Kyemap. "Oh, by the way, since you introduced me to my good fortune, you can come to my feast, too."

Kyemap gritted his teeth as he watched his cousin walk across the bare, dusty ground. A skinny dog got up and followed Poit to the edge of the village, then stopped and gazed sadly after the man. Finally, it turned around and wandered back, sniffing the ground for any potato peels Poit might have dropped. "I know just how you feel," Kyemap said, more to himself than the dog, "living off Poit's crumbs." He spat on the coals, making a loud sizzle. He didn't need a special invitation to Poit's feast. Anyone could go. It was tradition. But somehow Poit had a way of making Kyemap feel as unwelcome as a wildfire sweeping the Chaco's dry grass.

❖ ❖ ❖ ❖

Several months had passed without rain. Every water hole was dry, and only one of the mission wells had drinkable water. Pinse-Tawa, the witch doctor, decided he would try one more time to discredit the Christian God. After one Sunday's worship, he addressed Mr. Hunt in front of all the people.

"I have been trying to make rain," he said so everyone could hear, "but I cannot because everyone knows I need a new duck feather, and all the ducks have flown away." Then he turned to Mr. Hunt. "But you say that your God is good and kind to His children, that He hears your prayers, and that He is the one who sends the rain. Is that so?"

Mr. Hunt looked uneasy. "Yes."

"Then," said Pinse-Tawa, "why don't you pray to your God and ask for rain so our animals—and even we—won't die?"

Kyemap could see that Mr. Hunt was upset. "God does not like being tested," he said sharply. "But I will pray like the prophet Elijah that you will see God is more powerful than false gods."

Mr. Hunt prayed. He did not pray long, and he did not dance or yell or make a big show as the witch doctors did when they tried to get their spirits to help them. When he finished, he looked at Pinse-Tawa and then at the gathered villagers and simply said, "Now we will see."

The next afternoon, huge rain clouds gathered,

but no rain fell. However, that night it rained harder than Kyemap had ever remembered. In the morning every well was full. Every water hole was full. The rivers overflowed their banks. In fact, much of the Chaco had again become a vast swamp. And it was just the beginning of the rainy season.

As Kyemap splashed around in the puddles, he thought to himself that when Mr. Grubb returned, he would be ready to become a Christian.

❖ ❖ ❖ ❖

The next morning three visitors arrived at Waik. Kyemap was among many other villagers who gathered to see who they were. One was a red-faced man with a large stomach and straw hat. Like most foreign men, he had hair on his upper lip, but his mustache was whiter than his suit. A pair of spectacles hung from his collar by a gold chain.

The big man talked loudly and waved his arms as if he were trying to talk to someone on the other side of the river. Finally, he stopped talking and carefully looked from one to another of the mission houses as though examining which one he would choose. He pointed to the Hunts' house with its beautiful little flower garden that Mrs. Hunt tended so faithfully. Kyemap had never understood why she spent so much time growing flowers that no one could eat, but he did understand the fat man when he announced, "That one," and began walking toward it.

Andrew Pride quickly stepped in front of him,

shaking his head and saying, "No, no . . ." and many other words in English so fast and urgently that Kyemap did not understand them. Then he introduced the fat man to the Hunts. They shook hands, and finally they all headed off to Mr. Grubb's house.

All this while a small thin man followed the fat man and kept bowing to everyone like a swamp reed bending before a stiff breeze. He was a strange-looking fellow with a face like an armadillo—big ears, beady eyes, and a long, rough nose.

A third newcomer stood back by himself. He leaned against a tree with his legs crossed at the ankles and his arms folded across his chest. Kyemap watched an amused grin flicker across his face as he eyed the big man barking out orders to other people as he moved into Mr. Grubb's house.

The villagers were staring at the newcomers. Who were these men? Why had they come? Flustered, Andrew Pride came back out and announced in Lengua, "Please go to your homes. Come back this evening and we will introduce these visitors to everyone."

Chapter 6

The Lungfish Professor

WHEN THE MISSION BELL RANG just before sundown, everyone in the village gathered again in the now muddy field between the village and the mission. Mr. Pride raised his hand for their attention and spoke in the Lengua language. "As you know, we have some guests. This is Professor Kerr of Glasgow University in Scotland," he said, indicating the fat man in the white suit. "A professor is a very important teacher," he explained. "And this is his assistant, J. S. Budgett. They have come to study the lungfish."

Everyone was silent. What was a lungfish? "You know, the *lolach*!" Mr. Pride explained, using the Lengua word for the strange eel-like fish that grew abundantly in the swamps and rivers of the Chaco. It had both gills and lungs. When the swamps dried up—as they often did—the fish burrowed into the mud, leaving a little tube for air, and waited for rain. Some grew three feet in length.

The villagers looked at one another in puzzlement. Why would anyone want to study a lungfish? They caught the ugly creature all the time and ate it, but what could anyone learn from it? Quiet giggling broke out over such a silly idea and spread through the crowd until the people were openly laughing.

"Quiet, quiet, please," said Mr. Pride. "From time to time the professor may need your assistance in finding the fish or with other aspects of their research. I hope you will be willing to help."

Again the villagers laughed, but most also nodded their heads in agreement.

Kyemap then spoke up. "Has he seen Mr. Grubb?" he asked, and everyone became very quiet.

Mr. Pride said something to the visitors in English, and then he turned back toward the people. "Professor Kerr has not had the privilege of meeting with our Mr. Grubb, but this other fellow"—and he indicated the man who had held back that morning, smiling under the tree—"saw Mr. Grubb just before he left England. He is Robert Graham, a new missionary who is joining us."

"Has he drowned?" asked Kyemap.

Everyone looked at him in amazement. They were

probably wondering why he had asked such an unusual question. Finally, Mr. Pride said, "You must be concerned because he traveled so far across the sea." He repeated some words to Robert Graham in English. Both missionaries laughed, and then Mr. Pride addressed Kyemap. "Mr. Graham says that our Mr. Grubb is quite dry and well. No need to worry."

Kyemap sighed with relief as the crowd broke up and went back to their huts. Then he stopped and looked back. Mr. Grubb may be dry and well now, but he still had to come back across the salty sea. Would he drown then?

"Kyemap, wait," called Mr. Pride. Kyemap turned back. "You have worked closely with Mr. Grubb and the rest of us," said the missionary, "and you know a little English. Would you help Professor Kerr tomorrow?"

Kyemap shrugged. Why not?

The next morning, he arrived early to guide the fat professor and his assistant out onto the swamps and lagoons along the river where the lungfish could be found. Aware of the purpose of their trip, several other villagers volunteered to go along, too. With the recent rain, the lungfish would be coming out of their tunnels, and they would be very hungry and active. It would be a great day to catch lots of fish, and there would be a feast that evening.

But Professor Kerr needed more than a guide. He wanted to take all the comforts of home with him. Kyemap had to find two canoes the same size (which

wasn't easy) and lash them together, side by side.
Then he positioned a large chair with the right legs

resting in the bottom of the right canoe and the left legs in the left canoe. In front of this chair the professor wanted a small table. Overhead, Kyemap set up a large umbrella to give Professor Kerr shade—or protection from more rain, should it come. The professor also required writing materials, some large glass jars, and a pot of hot tea. The floating contraption was very unstable, but Kyemap did the best he could.

The sun was straight overhead before Kyemap pushed the craft off from shore using a pole to propel the professor and his floating "laboratory" out into the swamp. Mr. Budgett, the professor's assistant, paddled alongside in a dugout canoe of his own. But by that time of day, most of the other villagers were coming in, having caught all the fish they wanted.

Using sign language and the few English words Kyemap could understand, the professor asked how the fishing had gone that morning, so Kyemap translated. The report from the other fishermen was good, but no one held up their catch for the professor to see.

Unfortunately, Kyemap could not maneuver the canoes well enough to get close to any fish to spear them when they surfaced to breathe, and Mr. Budgett did not have the skill to do it himself. So after three unfruitful hours on the water, the discouraged professor indicated that he wanted to return to shore.

Walking stiffly after having sat so long, he finally waddled into the village, where cooking fires seemed to be going everywhere. Mr. Pride had no sooner joined them than the professor realized what was roasting over the fires. Huge lungfish were being turned on spits as they sizzled to a golden brown.

With a liveliness that surprised Kyemap, the professor began doing a foolish-looking dance from one cooking fire to another, waving his hands in the air and spinning around and shouting his foreign words.

"What's the matter with him? What's he saying?" asked Kyemap.

By then Mr. Pride was laughing so hard he had to hold his stomach. "He says," Pride gasped when he could catch his breath, "that he has come all the way from Europe to find these fish, and here you are cooking and eating the valuable creatures. They are larger, and there are more of them, than he ever imagined."

When the feast began, the professor shrugged as if to say, "Might as well join in," and accepted a roasted portion of fish on a large leaf. After a few bites he smacked his lips. With Mr. Pride translating, the professor explained that to the scientists in Europe, a lungfish was worth a month's wages. But now that he had found so many, and since they tasted so good, he might set up a canning factory right there on the Chaco and send canned lungfish back to England.

Yet when Mr. Pride had finished translating, he made a face and rolled his eyes. "I wouldn't pay a penny for a can of that fish," he added. "They taste like mud to me!"

As the weeks passed, Kyemap grew to resent being the professor's personal servant, always ordered about. "Find my slippers, boy." "Fetch me some tea." "Why weren't you here when I woke up this morning?" Kyemap had worked hard for Mr. Grubb, but Mr. Grubb had never taken advantage of him. But, he admitted to himself, there was one advantage to helping the professor: He was learning English. The professor did not know Lengua and made no attempt to learn it, so Kyemap had to do all the learning, and he learned fast.

✧ ✧ ✧ ✧

The thirteenth moon had come. Kyemap was worried. What would Mr. Grubb do when he returned—*if* he returned—and found someone else living in his house?

The day Grubb arrived back at the mission station in the middle of April 1897 was a glad day. Kyemap could hardly contain his excitement. Grubb hadn't drowned after all! And the day after his return, Mr. Pride left for his vacation.

"But why should I have to move into his house?" asked the professor when Mr. Grubb asked him how long it would take to get his things transferred into Pride's place. "Why should I move when all of my books and research are set up in your house. I would think that you could camp out in Pride's digs until I leave."

Mr. Grubb's eyebrow went up as if to ask whether

the professor now ran the whole mission station. Kyemap put his hand over his mouth and turned away.

"Because, Professor," said Mr. Grubb in an overly pleasant voice, "I have been 'camping out' for thirteen months, and I would like to get back into my 'digs,' as you call them, as soon as possible. The *work* of the mission is spreading the Gospel, not studying the lungfish, and so the Gospel must be our first task. You and your research efforts are welcome as long as it doesn't interfere."

With a look of innocent bewilderment on his face, the professor said, "But how would living in Pride's house for a while interfere with your preaching or whatever it is you do?"

"Look," said Grubb, "if you can't understand, then don't even ask. Get your stuff over to Pride's house by noon." Mr. Grubb walked away but then called back. "And by the way, you should prepare yourself. If the bishop or any other missionaries drop in on us for an extended stay, they will need Pride's house to stay in. We'll set you up in a tent."

❖ ❖ ❖

Several months passed at the mission station while Mr. Grubb used the Lengua dictionary that Mr. Hunt had been working on to prepare Bible lessons in the Lengua language. Kyemap was grateful that with Mr. Grubb's return, he no longer had to work for the professor. The professor was forced to hire various other Indians to help him make his trips gathering information about the lungfish and other creatures of the Chaco.

During this time, reports reached Waik that Poit had killed several of Mr. Grubb's cattle and had been providing nonstop feasts for anyone who wanted to attend. Kyemap was sure that Mr. Grubb must have heard the rumors, but the missionary never mentioned it to Kyemap.

One day Professor Kerr marched into the mission station sweating and as red as a dusty sunset. "You have a thief wandering around out there," he panted to Mr. Grubb. "And I want something done about it!"

"What are you talking about?" asked Mr. Grubb.

"I met some fellow on the trail who said he was a friend of yours," blurted Professor Kerr. "We were so shorthanded that I let him drive the cart, but then this morning when we broke camp, he had disappeared. And he took my new Winchester rifle with him!"

Mr. Grubb frowned. "How do you know?" he asked.

"I used it just yesterday to shoot at a peccary—a wild pig. I missed, but afterwards I put the rifle in the cart, and now it's gone," explained Kerr.

"Are you sure it didn't jostle out? It's pretty rough traveling out there," said Grubb.

"No, no. The case is still there—it's just the rifle that's missing. He took it; there's no other explanation," said Kerr.

"I'm sorry about your loss, Professor," said Mr. Grubb. "We'll put the word out. There are few enough guns here on the Chaco that if someone finds a Winchester and starts using it, word will soon get around."

The professor was not satisfied, but there wasn't anything he could do.

Later, when Mr. Grubb and Kyemap were planing lumber for a new medical clinic, Mr. Grubb asked, "What do you think about the professor's lost rifle? Has Poit come around lately?"

Kyemap shook his head. "I haven't seen him."

"What do you know about these rumors that he has given feasts?" he added.

Kyemap stopped his work and looked up. His cousin would be very angry if he told on him. "Who can tell about rumors?" he said. After thinking for a few moments he added, "He told me that he thought you were dead. Maybe he thought the cattle were his."

Mr. Grubb stopped planing the wood. "But I'm not dead! I came back in thirteen months, just like I promised. If he has killed some of my cattle, he's going to have to—" He did not finish his threat.

After a few moments, Kyemap spoke again. "Maybe that's why he hasn't come to see you. He's probably afraid."

Chapter 7

Dead Man Walking

PROFESSOR KERR and his funny-looking assistant finally left the Chaco and returned to England. They were happy with all the research they had done on lungfish. However, Mr. Grubb did not think they would be back to set up a fish canning factory.

Weeks later, Kyemap was sweeping the steps when Poit and three strange Indians walked up to the missionary's house. "Well, if it isn't my favorite cousin," Poit announced. "You still working here for nothing?"

Kyemap stopped sweeping and wiped the back of his hand across his sweaty forehead. If he was Poit's "favorite," he'd hate to see how Poit treated an unpopular cousin.

Mr. Grubb came out onto the porch, letting the screen door slam behind him. Kyemap looked around to see a frown on his face. "Poit!" Grubb said gruffly. "I hear that you—"

"Mr. Grubb!" Poit interrupted. "Mr. Grubb, I have brought you three Toothli Indians who would like you to come visit their tribe in the West."

Mr. Grubb's frown melted into a smile. "Toothli Indians? Welcome! Welcome! Kyemap, would you please go make tea for everyone? Then come and join us under the mesquite trees out back."

Kyemap shook his head as he walked into the house. Poit's diversion had worked. That rascal could get away with anything. Kyemap knelt down and opened the door on the small black iron stove and blew on the coals. Then he checked to see that there was enough water in the kettle on top.

A few minutes later, when he went out to the chairs under the trees carrying the tray with a pot of tea and cups for everyone, Poit was in busy conversation with Mr. Grubb, translating what the Toothlis were saying . . . or that was what he was claiming to do. But who knew? Maybe his cousin was making it all up in order to interest Mr. Grubb and keep him from asking about the cattle or the professor's rifle. The Lengua and the Toothli languages were similar, but Kyemap could only understand a few words, and it was obvious that Mr. Grubb couldn't catch any of it.

75

The Toothli visitors had to leave that afternoon. But it was decided that as soon as Mr. Grubb could make arrangements, he and Poit would travel west to visit the Toothli people. "Tell them that we'll stop on the way at Namuk and pick up some of my cattle and bring them as gifts," Mr. Grubb said, smiling at the Toothli men.

Kyemap was watching Poit and saw his face turn gray and his eyes flicker with fear at the mention of cattle. But Poit recovered quickly and began speaking to the visitors using a lot of excited hand gestures. Again, Kyemap could not follow what he said, but he did not hear the word "cow," which he should have been able to recognize, even in the Toothli langauge.

✧ ✧ ✧ ✧

A disease had recently killed many of the horses in that part of the Chaco, and those who hadn't died had been greatly weakened by the disease. Mr. Grubb decided that the trip to the West should be made on foot. But at the Sunday service when he said that he wanted to hire several Indians to help carry supplies, the villagers began urging him not to go. One old woman stood up and said sadly, "Please, Mr. Grubb, I have had a dream about you. If you go to the West, you will leave your bones along the road to whiten in the sun."

"Thank you for your concern," said the missionary kindly, "but you know I don't believe in superstitious dreams. This is an important trip to reach the

Toothli tribe. Poit will be my guide, but I need five more men to carry supplies. Today is December 12 and I want to get going tomorrow. Who will go with me?"

Reluctantly, five men raised their hands, but as the villagers left the service, several were shaking their heads and muttering, "He should not go. He has been traveling too much and should stay home."

Light was just spreading up the eastern sky when Kyemap arrived at Mr. Grubb's house the next morning. The idea was to get in as much traveling as they could before the hot sun forced them to stop. But when the missionary came out onto his porch, he said, "I'm sorry, Kyemap, but you will not be going with me this time. Robert Graham needs help with the Lengua language. I know he's new, but he seems to be having an awful time. You could be a big help to him."

Kyemap didn't mean to make a face at the missionary's request, but he was tired of "lessons"! Even in the gray dawn Mr. Grubb must have seen his displeasure because he quickly added, "You don't have to sit around with him as though you were in a class. He needs help in the mission store; someone stole $28 from there the other day. So just answer his questions, and for goodness' sake, help him get his accent right. He talks like he has a chicken bone in his mouth."

Half an hour later, Kyemap watched with a heavy face and sagging shoulders as his cousin gave orders to the other Indians about what order they should walk in—with himself in the lead beside Mr. Grubb, of course—and how they had all better "keep up" or he would withhold their pay. Kyemap's eyes narrowed. How had *he* become boss? Then the little procession headed out of Waik until their blue shadows disappeared into the rosy mists of the early Chaco morning.

✧ ✧ ✧ ✧

Nine days later as Kyemap was closing up the little store in the evening, a messenger came running into the mission station from the direction of

the setting sun. He had been running so long and hard that he collapsed on the ground and was barely able to gasp, "News! . . . Grubb . . . dead!"

Kyemap had no idea how the word spread, but within moments all the missionaries and thirty or forty villagers had gathered around the sweating man who had finally raised himself to a sitting position as he panted for breath.

Robert Graham was pulling on Kyemap's arm. "What did he say? I couldn't understand him. What did he say?"

In his faltering English, Kyemap told the new missionary what the man had said.

"What do you mean, 'dead'?" demanded Richard Hunt, bending over the runner. "How can that be?" Then, because their house was closest, he turned to his wife. "Mary, would you fetch a cup of water? The man has exhausted himself."

"Are you sure it was Grubb?" said Sibeth, the cart driver.

Once Mrs. Hunt brought the water and the man drank a little, he tried to explain. "Somewhere in Jaguar Swamp . . ." he panted for more air, " . . . possibly twenty-five miles west of Poit's village, . . . Namuk, . . . not far from Toothli territory . . ." He stopped and reached again for the cup of water.

"Just tell us what happened, man!" demanded Mr. Hunt.

"Jaguar! Grubb and Poit were attacked by a jaguar," he blurted.

"But how did you find out?" said Hunt.

The man was finally recovering his breath. "Poit—he managed to escape. But Grubb died, and Poit was unable to retrieve his body from the huge cat."

A great hubbub went through the growing crowd. Sibeth growled, "If he didn't get his body, how can Poit be sure Grubb was dead? Maybe he was just badly injured. Maybe he needs help. Did anyone else go out to check?"

"I don't know," said the messenger, starting to cough. "All I know"—*cough, cough*—"is what the last runner told me."

"Well, I'm going after him!" declared Sibeth. "If there is any chance of retrieving his body for burial, someone has to go."

"Me too," added Robert Graham.

Dozens of the villagers joined in, saying that they were going, too. They would catch that "deceitful Poit," as they called him, and find out why he hadn't taken better care of *their* Mr. Grubb. But the missionaries urged them to calm down and wait patiently. They had only heard the first report from the scene, and no one knew for sure what had happened. Sibeth and Graham could handle whatever needed doing.

This time Kyemap decided that he was not going to be left behind.

There were only two horses left in the mission station that were healthy enough to ride, and sometimes, when the fever struck them, even they wobbled like newborn colts. It was midnight when Sibeth and Graham rode out of Waik. Kyemap watched from the shadows of the huts at the edge of the village until they were out of sight, and then he followed quietly.

It was not hard to keep up with the weak horses, but Kyemap kept his distance until dawn when Graham and Sibeth arrived at Paisiam. Chief Mechi and all the villagers came out of their huts to see if the foreigners had any more news. Graham and Sibeth, of course, were wondering the same of the villagers. Sibeth knew the Lengua language better than Graham, but still there were immediate problems of communication. That's when Kyemap stepped forward.

"Kyemap! What are you doing here?" asked Graham.

"I thought you might use some help translating," suggested Kyemap. "So I followed along."

The two foreigners frowned but quickly asked Kyemap if the villagers had any more news about Mr. Grubb.

There was no new information about Mr. Grubb, but someone did say that Poit was traveling toward them. "He is on his way back to Waik," said the villager. "If you hurry, you may be able to meet him at the village of Mopai by nightfall."

Mopai was another thirty-five miles west. Tired as they were, the possibility of hearing directly from Poit about what had happened urged Sibeth, Graham, and Kyemap on. As they left Paisiam, Kyemap looked with longing at Chief Mechi's horse in its palm-shaded coral. It was the healthiest-looking horse he'd seen on the Chaco since the horse disease had come, but the chief did not offer it for him to ride. Probably he knew three couldn't ride one horse, and Kyemap could certainly walk as fast as the weakened beasts Sibeth and Graham rode.

✧ ✧ ✧ ✧

Kyemap had never walked so far in one day in his entire life. When the party from Waik finally straggled into Mopai, several people gathered around them, but it was an old woman who offered information. "Yes, yes. Poit is here, but he is hiding in a hut and will not talk to anyone." Then, after a long pause her wrinkled face brightened, and she waved her finger from side to side. "But Mr. Grubb is not dead!"

"W-what?" stammered Kyemap.

"He is not dead—not yet!" she added.

This information created a great deal of confusion as Kyemap tried to get the story straight and explain it to Graham and Sibeth. Apparently, said the woman, Mr. Grubb had been severely wounded but had managed to crawl to a trail where an Indian found him and took him to a village on the Lengua frontier. "But he will die soon," said the women solemnly. She had gotten her information from a second news runner who had arrived after Poit. "Mr. Grubb lost much, much blood. He is not dead yet, but by now, he is no more than a dead man walking."

She then led the three people from Waik along with several local people to the hut where Poit was hiding. Kyemap could hardly believe what he found

82

inside. The filthy, wide-eyed creature that cowered in the corner looked very little like his proud elder cousin. For some time, Poit only grunted responses to their questions.

"Come on, now, man," urged Graham, "speak up. Is Mr. Grubb dead or alive?"

After Kyemap translated the question for the fifth time, Poit finally said, "He *was* dead."

"What do you mean, 'He *was* dead'? They say he is alive. They say he crawled away. Why did you leave him?" pressed Sibeth in an angry voice.

"I *thought* he was dead," pleaded Poit like a whimpering child. "I saw him go down. There was nothing I could do."

After Kyemap translated, Sibeth shouted, "Why didn't you get some Indians from the next village and go back for him?"

"I don't know! I don't know!" protested Poit. "I was afraid. . . . I didn't know where I was. I barely escaped with my own life. The jaguar was very fierce!"

"Jaguar?" said the old woman, who was still standing in the entrance to the hut. "The runner didn't say anything about a jaguar. He said Mr. Grubb had been shot in the back with an arrow!"

Chapter 8

Ghost of the Chaco

N O, NO!" POIT PROTESTED in a panic-stricken voice. "That can't be true. We were attacked by the jaguar."

Sibeth understood enough of this answer not to need translation. "Then where are your arrows?" he demanded, pointing at the bow that lay in the dust beside Poit.

In the dim light of the hut, Poit frowned as though he was trying to remember something. Then he began speaking as though he were in a dream. "I had five arrows . . . yes, five arrows, and I shot them all at the jaguar." But the more he  spoke, the more excited he became. "I wounded that great cat, making it all the more dangerous—that's why I couldn't go to Grubb's aid. I had no weapon!" he said as though he had finally discovered the answer to an important puzzle.

"But if Mr. Grubb was wounded by an arrow in the back," challenged Graham, "then it must have come from you. *You* shot him, and if he dies, you will have killed him!"

"No, no, no!" protested Poit as he dissolved into sobs. "I couldn't have killed him."

They talked on and on with the confused Poit until he finally admitted that one of his arrows *might* have hit Grubb accidentally. "But by then," he protested, "he was so severely mauled by the jaguar that it wouldn't have made any difference. He was dying. What could I do?"

"What could you do?" said Kyemap with disgust. "The least you could have done was to go for help." It was the first comment Kyemap had made on his own that had not been the translation of another's question.

Poit jumped to his feet. With hands on his hips and his nose just inches from Kyemap's face, he snapped, "Who are you to challenge me, you half-grown grasshopper? I did not kill Mr. Grubb! The jaguar killed him, and I did everything I could to defend him. I shot all my arrows at that enormous cat. The cat was wounded by my arrows, and everyone knows that it is impossible to approach a wounded cat!"

With that he pushed his way through the people and out the door of the hut. As he stalked through the dusty village, his pace got faster and faster until he ran out the other side and into the forest north of Mopai.

✧ ✧ ✧ ✧

It was Saturday, Christmas day, when the three from Waik—hoping now to be Mr. Grubb's rescuers—arrived at Namuk, Poit's village. Poit, of course, was not there. He had disappeared into the jungle, but the rescuers didn't care because they were looking for Mr. Grubb.

"Yes, yes," the villagers said, "Mr. Grubb slept here last night. He came to us staggering—sometimes crawling—from a village many miles west of here, but he would not stay with us. He insisted he had to get back to Waik. We gave him our only remaining horse. It could barely walk, and so we sent two men to walk alongside to keep Mr. Grubb from falling off. But . . . he will die soon," they said sadly, and everyone nodded their heads in sad agreement.

"Something's not right," said Graham after hearing the villager's story. "They are not telling the truth. How could we have missed Mr. Grubb if he were on his way to Waik? We have just come from that direction."

But when Kyemap questioned the villagers, they pointed down a different trail. "It was getting so hot, that our old horse could never have traveled across the open Chaco. So we sent Mr. Grubb through the forest."

It was a likely explanation. The temperature had

already climbed to 110 degrees in the shade. Without taking time for rest or refreshment, the rescue party headed down the trail indicated by the villagers.

Walking ahead of the missionaries, Kyemap found fresh hoofprints on the forest trail. "They can't be far ahead now!" he announced to Sibeth and Graham following behind on the sickly horses, whose heads hung almost to the ground.

Ten minutes later, they came out of the trees and into a marsh with grass that was five feet high. "Can you see them?" asked Kyemap anxiously.

Sibeth stood in his stirrups, looking out across the plain. "No," he said. "How could they have disappeared? . . . No, wait! . . . I see something, straight ahead! Grubb must be down, because the grass hid them all."

They hurried forward to an opening where a wheezing horse, down on its side, had flattened the grass. A couple feet away were three men. Mr. Grubb sat in the ankle-deep marsh water with an Indian supporting him on either side. Blood and drool dripped from his mouth as he coughed weakly, trying to get his breath.

Kyemap arrived at his side only seconds before Graham and Sibeth had time to drop from their horses and sprint the last few yards.

"We're here; we're here, brother," Andrew Graham said in English as he replaced the Indian on the other side of Grubb.

Grubb looked hollowly from one to the other of

his rescuers. Feebly, he pointed to Kyemap on one side as he spoke to Graham on his other side, "Hasn't . . . this boy . . . taught you Lengua yet? What have you two . . . been doing with your time?" His weak laugh at his own joke turned into a coughing fit that brought up more blood.

✧ ✧ ✧ ✧

Somehow the rescue party managed to get Grubb back on one of the horses, and they returned to Namuk, where they tried to make him as comfortable as possible. He had only one wound, a deep and terrible hole in his back that looked far more like an arrow wound than anything a jaguar could have done. When Kyemap pointed this out to Graham and Sibeth, they shook their heads. "Let's not question him about what happened just now," said Sibeth. "There'll be time enough for that later . . . if we can get him safely back to Waik."

They couldn't have questioned Mr. Grubb if they had wanted to, because by then he was losing consciousness and mumbling gibberish. "We've got to get him back to Waik," said Graham. "He needs medicines and clean bandages."

"At least let him rest until tomorrow," said Sibeth. Kyemap volunteered to stay with Mr. Grubb the remainder of that day and all during the night, bathing him when his fever raged and comforting him with hot rocks wrapped in blankets when he shivered from chill.

Kyemap did not sleep all night, but in the early dawn when Mr. Grubb slept peacefully for the first time, Kyemap left the hut to stretch his legs. Outside, he noticed one of the village hunters talking to a friend and showing off a small bag of money. Could this man be the thief who had stolen the money from the mission store? Kyemap had never seen him at Waik. Nevertheless, he casually walked over to the man and asked, "How did someone way back here in the bush get so much money?"

"It walks across the Chaco," the hunter said through a wide, toothless grin.

"Traveling money, huh?" Kyemap observed. "How much is it?"

The man shrugged but agreeably leaned down and dumped out the coins on a split log. Kyemap quickly counted the coins and realized that they amounted to exactly twenty-eight dollars. "Were you ever at Waik?" he asked.

The man shook his head solemnly.

"Then where did you get this white man's money?"

The hunter just laughed and said, "I sold my iron-tipped arrows, all five of them." Then he walked away.

Kyemap did not have time to consider what this meant because Sibeth was calling to him. Knowing that their two sick horses were almost spent, and fearing that Mr. Grubb might not be able to stay astride a horse anyway, Sibeth had built a travois to carry him. "What do you think of this?" he asked as he led his tired horse to the front of the hut in which

Mr. Grubb slept. Two long poles were tied to the saddle, one on each side and dragging on the ground behind. A blanket was tied to the two poles like a stretcher.

Kyemap agreed that it was better than trying to keep Grubb on a horse. "But the going will be slower," he said.

"Not any slower than if this horse gives out . . . or Grubb falls off," Sibeth added.

❖ ❖ ❖ ❖

A long day of hard travel brought the bedraggled party to Mopai. Grubb didn't seem to be any worse, but he still hadn't regained his senses enough to know where he was. He did seem to know that he was with friends, though, and often reached out a feeble hand to take comfort in their touch.

After two more days of slow travel, the party arrived at Paisiam. From the point of his attack, Grubb had traveled over ninety miles in his weakened condition. "Hang on, you can make it," encouraged Robert Graham as he walked alongside the missionary. "We'll spend the night here, and tomorrow there'll be only another fifteen miles to go before we get you to the mission station."

But as they entered Paisiam, Kyemap noticed a strange response from the villagers. They all crowded around the slowly-moving travois, but the moment they saw Mr. Grubb, they drew back, some holding their hands over their mouths, others staring at the missionary from a distance. A few even ran to their huts and disappeared inside.

Kyemap looked at Mr. Grubb. His eyes were closed as his head rocked slowly back and forth with the motion of the travois, and his pale face was covered by the dark stubble of a short beard—that strange feature of foreigners—but Kyemap didn't think he looked *that* bad.

Then Chief Mechi came alongside the travois. He stared at Grubb a long time, walking just slower than the horse so that distance increased between himself and the injured missionary. Finally, he turned to Kyemap and said, "Is it really Mr. Grubb?"

"Of course," said Kyemap. "Who else could he be?"

The chief looked this way and that. "Who knows? Mr. Grubb *was* dead, wasn't he? We all heard the reports." Then the chief added confidentially, "Maybe some other spirit took over his body. Maybe . . . he is a ghost!"

Chapter 9

The Iron Arrow

WISPS OF A MERCILESS CHACO BREEZE brushed Kyemap's face like hot feathers as the rescue party plodded into Waik shortly before sunset.

"Did I miss Christmas?" whispered Mr. Grubb from his rickety travois.

"I'm afraid so," said Sibeth. "It's December 29, but you're finally home, so rest easy."

Just as in Paisiam, the villagers of Waik quickly gathered around and elbowed one another aside to get a look at what appeared to float in a little swirl of dust behind the frail horse. Again Kyemap heard the hushed word "ghost" muttered from one person to another as they shrank back from the shadow of a man on the travois.

For two days Kyemap nursed Mr. Grubb before he seemed to fully recover his senses. On New Year's Day the other missionaries and a few of the Indian elders gathered at Mr. Grubb's bedside. "Grubb, can you tell us what happened in the swamp?" Richard Hunt asked. Kyemap noticed that one of the five carriers who had started the trip with Mr. Grubb and Poit had come with the little group.

Mr. Grubb frowned, as though trying to remember. "From early on," he said, "things didn't go right. We were only a short distance beyond Mopai when for some reason our five Indian carriers lagged behind." He took a sip of water from the glass that Kyemap had placed on the small table beside his bed. "I didn't think much of it. It was hot, and they had heavy loads, so I thought they were picking some fruit or something. Finally, however, about noon, I sat down under a tree and sent Poit back to hurry them up.

"For some reason, Poit took a long time, and when he finally came back, he had a little food and my tea kettle, but no carriers followed him. 'One of them ran a long thorn into his foot,' Poit told me. 'They'll catch us by evening.'"

"But . . . that's not right!" said the carrier. "Poit told us to go back to Mopai and wait there. He said it might be two weeks before you came back for us."

"He told you what?" said Mr. Grubb. "But why would we have hired you as carriers only to dismiss you when we were just halfway there? Unless . . ." His voice trailed off.

The Indian carrier raised his palms in a helpless manner. "We couldn't understand why you didn't need your supplies or would go on alone, but Poit said those were your instructions, so . . . we went back."

"Yes, I'm beginning to see," said Grubb.

Richard Hunt leaned forward, putting his elbows on his knees and folding his hands. "Then what happened?" he asked.

"Well, of course the carriers didn't catch up that night, and I was rather upset. But Poit said not to worry. We went on until a couple days later we got to his village, Namuk. The first thing I wanted to do was check my cattle, but Poit kept putting me off, saying they were out to pasture and it would take too long to round them up. I guess I became upset, because I told him to have his relatives round up all the cattle by the time we returned or he would be in big trouble."

Mr. Grubb stopped, and Kyemap adjusted his pillow so he could sit up better. Then he continued. "The next morning I had Poit recruit some men from his village and some sweet potatoes and manioc and other items for trading, and we headed on west to the last Lengua village on the frontier. But that night I had a touch of malaria fever, and the next morning Poit suggested not leaving until the dew was off the swamp grass. We were very close to Jaguar Swamp by then. He sent the new carriers on ahead.

"While we were eating breakfast, I noticed that he had some new iron-tipped arrows and asked him about them. 'Oh, Mr. Grubb,' he said, 'this is jaguar country. My wooden arrows would never do if we met a big cat. So I traded them for these fine arrows back at Namuk.'"

Grubb took several deep breaths, and the listeners waited patiently till he was ready to go on. "Finally," he said, "we got under way, but it was already getting hot. Several times we crossed the river Monte until I asked Poit if he knew where he was going. It seemed like he was getting us lost. 'This is a shortcut,' he said. Still weak from the malaria attack, I was a little short-tempered and told him that if this was a shortcut, I'd rather stay on the trail. I was tired of tramping through bush and swamp.

"But I didn't know the way, so there was nothing to do but keep going. Eventually we entered a forest, but soon the undergrowth got so dense that our path was blocked. Poit then left me, saying he would scout a better trail. A short time later I heard something crackling branches in the thicket ahead, and I began making a lot of noise to scare away whatever it was, especially if it was a jaguar."

"Make noise?" injected Robert Graham, the newest missionary at the station. "I'd be inclined to keep silent and hope no wild animal would find me."

Sibeth snorted. "You never want to surprise a dangerous animal. Most wild animals prefer to get away from humans, but if you surprise one, it's likely to attack, thinking it is defending itself from you. No, making noise was the right thing."

"Yes," said Grubb absently. "Anyway, the crackling stopped, but then in a few minutes I saw Poit looking at me through the thicket with a very strange expression on his face. For a moment I wondered whether he had seen a jaguar, but then he said, 'The trail is clear over this way. Just push on through. It won't take long.' And he disappeared from sight into the foliage.

"After that, I tried to get through the thicket, but it was impossible. Then Poit called out again, 'Wait, I'll come help you.' I kept pushing at the tangle of vines and bushes until I felt this terrible blow to my back. It was so hard that it would have knocked me flat to the ground if the brush hadn't caught me.

"I struggled to regain my footing, I turned around to see Poit standing about five yards behind me with his bow in his hand. Then he yelled, 'Oh my! Oh my!' and ran off toward the river." Grubb stared off into space for a moment and then added, "I never saw him again."

"But was there a jaguar?" demanded Mr. Hunt, pointing his finger toward Mr. Grubb and tipping his head to the side as he asked the most crucial question.

Grubb shrugged. "I don't know, but . . . I don't think so. On the other hand, everything in my memory is a little fuzzy about what happened next."

"But obviously Poit shot you," said Hunt, "so the question is, why?"

"If there was a jaguar, and Poit shot at it, I suppose he could have accidentally shot me . . ." Grubb mused.

As everyone began discussing the possibility of whether Poit had been trying to shoot a jaguar or not or whether there even was a jaguar, Kyemap stepped away from the bed and stared through the screen that surrounded the sleeping porch. He frowned. There might have been a reason for Poit to shoot Grubb. He had told Kyemap that Grubb's cattle belonged to him now, and there had been rumors of big feasts. Also, Grubb said that when they went through Namuk, Poit made an excuse for not producing the herd for inspection. Was Poit so afraid of being found out about stealing Grubb's cattle that he decided to kill Mr. Grubb?

The thought seemed impossible! As much as Poit got on Kyemap's nerves, and even though Poit was a very selfish person, Kyemap could hardly believe his cousin would stoop to murder. That was too much . . . or was it?

Suddenly, Kyemap realized that Mr. Grubb was continuing his story. He turned back just as Grubb was saying, "That arrow was stuck in my back so deep that I couldn't pull it out. And when I tried to reach back there, the pain was so bad that I nearly passed out. I staggered along by the river's edge not knowing what to do until I came to this little sapling that had a Y about chest high. I finally worked myself around until I got the shaft of that arrow wedged between the two branches of that little sapling. When I was sure it was really caught, I just lunged forward and let myself fall.

"The pain was so great that I blacked out. When I

woke up, blood was all over me, and I was coughing up more. I knew right then that my lung had been punctured, and I thought for sure that I was dead. But I couldn't just give up and die. I cried out to God to see me through, and then I began crawling."

"Excuse me," said Kyemap. "Did you get a look at that arrow?"

"Oh yes," Grubb said, his eyes going wide. "It was a wicked one, an iron-tipped arrow—one of those he had traded his own arrows for, I suppose. That arrowhead was nearly seven inches long, and the tip had bent over, probably where it had hit my bone. I suppose that's why it was so hard to pull out."

Everyone groaned.

"Anyway," continued Grubb, "I crawled on until I came to the river's edge. There was nowhere to turn, so I had to go through. The cool water refreshed me somewhat, but I kept worrying that if I fainted again, I would certainly drown, so I hung on until I came up on the other side. I struggled on through the forest for I don't know how long until I came across a trail, and then I collapsed. I didn't pass out, but I literally couldn't muster enough strength to go farther.

"But God was with me, because within an hour a man came jogging down the trail. He was returning home to his village—the very one we had stayed in the night before. He recognized me and helped lean me up against a tree and then went for help. Before long several kind villagers arrived and made a stretcher to carry me back to the village."

Robert Graham blew air through his lips as

though he had been holding his breath for the last of the story. "I'm sure you were glad that ordeal was over," he said. "Thank God!"

"Thank God, indeed," said Grubb, "but I was far from being out of danger."

"What do you mean?" said Graham. "You said those people were very friendly."

"They were, but the Lengua people are also very superstitious." Grubb took another sip of water. "I was in danger from two of their beliefs. First, they believe that anyone who passes out is dead, so I was even afraid to fall asleep. What if they couldn't wake me? Second, they believe if a person dies in their village at night, his ghost will haunt their village, and they have to move. Isn't that right, Kyemap?"

Kyemap dropped his head. "Yes, sir," he mumbled. Then he looked up at the other people around Grubb's bed. Why should he feel embarrassed about such superstitions? They were not of his making. In a matter-of-fact tone he added, "My grandmother was buried when she was still awake because the witch doctor said she would die that night, and no one wanted her to die in the village after dark." Then he grinned at Mr. Grubb. "But I don't believe in ghosts anymore."

"I sure could have used a few people like you in that village!" said Grubb. "No one even knew how to clean my wound." He paused as though recalling events. "One of the first things I did when I was clearheaded enough to think was send a messenger back here to Waik to tell you about my state. I was so grateful when you three came for me!

"Now, where was I in my story? Oh yes. As you can imagine, I didn't get much rest that night. The next day many people came to visit me, even from neighboring villages. Everyone shook their heads and said they had never seen anyone with such a severe wound who survived—not very encouraging, I can tell you. But they meant no harm." Grubb chuckled. "They told me they intended to take the best possible care of me. They had even selected a beautiful spot under a nice shade tree for my last resting place. That evening, the children kept coming up to me and saying, 'It's getting dark. Are you strong?' You can believe that I did some very serious praying that nothing would happen during the night to make them think that I had lost consciousness. Though I napped a little that night, I did not permit myself to fall into a deep sleep.

"The next morning I forced myself to begin traveling east. I was so dizzy that if I hadn't had the help of some kind Indians, I'm certain that I would have wandered in circles. Sometimes I walked. Sometimes I rested. One of the Indians even offered to carry me on his back, but that didn't work. Finally, with the Lord's help, I made it to Namuk, which is where Sibeth, Graham, and Kyemap found me. And—well, you know the rest."

As Mr. Grubb ended his story, the conversation once again turned to why Poit might have shot Mr. Grubb. Had he missed the jaguar and hit Grubb by accident? Had there even been a jaguar? If not, it looked as though the shooting was intentional, but no one could think of why he would do such a thing. Still, Poit had run off. Why?

There was only one way to solve the mystery: find Poit and get the truth from him!

Chapter 10

The Manhunt

WHILE THE OTHER PEOPLE around Mr. Grubb's bed discussed Poit's motives and whereabouts, Kyemap wandered out the front door. *He* could think of a motive for why Poit might have shot Mr. Grubb! Poit hadn't wanted him to find out about the cattle he had killed and the feasts he had held.

In fact, Kyemap had an idea of who had taken the money from the mission store and why. It all fit together! Poit had stolen the money from the mission store to buy the iron-tipped arrows. Then he tried to kill Mr. Grubb to cover his greed in taking the missionary's cattle.

But as much as Kyemap disliked Poit, he was his cousin. Kyemap couldn't condemn his own relative without being absolutely sure of his guilt.

He sat down on the bottom step of Mr. Grubb's house, which creaked loudly with his weight. The cicadas were whining in the nearby mesquite trees, and the air smelled like rain might finally fall from the gold and gray thunderheads that boiled in the sky over the Chaco.

Kyemap picked up a mesquite pod, snapped it open, and began gnawing absently at the sweet pulp inside. Finding Poit could be a problem. He traveled so much that he might have a dozen places to hide. There might even be whole villages that would protect him.

Suddenly, Kyemap threw down the remains of the mesquite pod and got up. There was one place he could look, a place no one else knew about—Poit's private "hunting lodge," the bottle trunk tree he had hollowed out down near the Sievo River. Could he find it again?

Saying nothing to anyone about where he was going, Kyemap stopped by his hut to pick up his drinking gourd, then headed out of the village and across the Chaco.

✧ ✧ ✧ ✧

The heavy, damp air felt exhausted. After hours of trying, it had failed to wring any rain from the clouds that were now breaking up in the West to reveal a sunset that looked like pink rose petals thrown on a blue pond. Kyemap slowed his easy jog to a walk. He recognized the grassy plain that bordered the Sievo River. Just a short distance upstream he would find the bottle trunk tree Poit used for his hunting lodge. The sharp grass stung his legs. He would welcome a rest at Poit's hidden lodge.

But when he finally saw the lone tree with its bulbous trunk and spindly, crooked limbs sprayed out from the top of the trunk, he hesitated. What if Poit were hiding there now and didn't want to be found—by anyone? He might be very angry that Kyemap had come. And if Poit had actually tried to kill Mr. Grubb, would he become violent if Kyemap confronted his cousin about the shooting?

The young Indian observed the tree from a distance. There was no smoke coming out of the dark gash down one side, and Kyemap did not see any personal belongings scattered about outside. He waited for a long time, then slowly circled to get a better view.

"Poit, you there?" he called in a tentative voice. He shivered—even though the air was as heavy as steam from a stew pot—and took a few more steps. "Poit?"

There was no response.

He waited fifteen minutes, then half an hour as the sky cleared and the pink clouds that had streaked the West faded to gray. The light on the Chaco dimmed, washing out the browns, yellows, greens, blacks, and whites until everything was either a lighter or darker shade of the same blue. Kyemap crept closer, bending low and letting the tall grass and occasional bush hide his body, and still there was no sign of Poit. He called once more, then stood up straight and looked all around the clearing. Either his cousin was there or not. It was time to find out. He walked directly toward the peculiar tree.

As he put his hand against the tree, he said, "Poit?" one last time before sticking his head into the opening, but by then he knew no one was there. The grass outside had not been trampled by any recent traffic.

Inside there was just enough room for a man to squat down. Kyemap felt around in the dark. Some hunting lodge! Anyone who spent the night in a place as small as this would be so cramped the next morning that a snail could outrun him.

Then Kyemap felt something cold and hard and long. It was metal. It was heavy. Carefully, he picked it up and held it in the dim light that came through the entrance. A rifle. Kyemap rolled it from side to side in his hand, feeling the balance of the gun. Cautiously, he cocked the lever downward under the handle. The rifle was empty. He felt around on the floor of the hiding place and then on the walls in case a bag of ammunition was hanging there. Nothing!

He stepped outside and looked around the clearing as though he expected Poit to return any moment. Then in the better light, he examined the rifle again. He had seen its custom engraved side panels

before. It was Professor Kerr's new Winchester rifle, with tiny specs of rust already etching their way into its blue barrel.

Kyemap looked back at the entrance in the bottle trunk tree. The evidence appeared even worse for Poit. Had he stolen the professor's rifle thinking he would kill Mr. Grubb with it only to find it had no bullets in it? When that didn't work out, had he taken money from the mission store in order to purchase the next best weapon, the iron-tipped arrows? "Oh, cousin, I hope this is not true," Kyemap said to the still evening air. "Selfish as you are, I cannot believe you would commit murder!"

Was there any way to prove that Poit had not intended to shoot Mr. Grubb? Had he bought the arrows, as he said, as protection from the jaguar?

Kyemap looked up at the purple sky. A bright moon, two nights beyond first quarter, was just rising. In spite of the clouds that often came up in the afternoons, it had not rained for over a week, since before Mr. Grubb was shot. If it had not rained in the West, either, then there still ought to be tracks in the soft, swampy ground where the shooting had occurred. Jaguars were big, heavy cats. If one had been there, ready to attack Mr. Grubb as Poit claimed, it would leave tracks, and those tracks should still be visible.

He would go and find proof for what really happened. If it was an accident, he would prove it.

✧ ✧ ✧ ✧

When Kyemap arrived at Paisiam, only a few miles from Poit's bottle trunk tree, most of the men were already out looking for Poit. It seemed like the whole Lengua people had been alerted that Poit was a wanted man. The missionaries had only wanted to question him, but as Kyemap listened to the Indians talk, it was obvious that many of them considered him guilty of murder.

When Kyemap heard the word "murder" mentioned by a group of women—and a few old men—

who were gossiping around a common fire, he slipped away into the dark shadows of the village. This was becoming serious. If Poit were caught and found to be guilty of murder, he could be sentenced to death. If that happened, the Lengua custom was to also kill all immediate family members. It was a harsh but effective way to prevent feuds—no one was left alive who cared enough to take revenge on the executioners.

A knot of fear pinched his stomach. It was unlikely that the elimination of family members would reach as far as Kyemap's family, he reasoned—they weren't that closely related to Poit. But during the past year Kyemap himself had spent a lot of time with Poit. Once people had drunk enough strong beer, it was never certain where the killing would stop. They might think he was close enough to Poit that he would want to take revenge. His life could be in danger, too.

The moon lit his way as Kyemap wove through the village huts until he came to Chief Mechi's home. The old chief was more levelheaded than many people, and Kyemap hoped he could trust him with his plan. "Chief Mechi?" he called softly from outside the hut. "Chief Mechi?"

Someone stirred inside and came to pull back the dusty blanket that served as a door. In the soft moonlight, Kyemap could see the pearly cataracts that blinded the old chief's eyes. "Who is it?" he said.

"I am Kyemap. I come from Yitlo-yimmaling, a very small village in the West, but I think you know my father. He used to hunt with you for tapirs every year."

"Oh yes. Come in," he said, holding back the blanket. "I'm sorry I have no candle or fire. Light doesn't help me much anymore, at least not in my own hut."

Kyemap tripped over a water jug before he found a seat on a mat near the chief's bed. After a respectful silence, he said, "I have come to beg your help and the use of your fine horse. It is the only way I can make the long trip I must make in time to be of any good."

Then he told of his plan to travel west to the site where Mr. Grubb had been shot and see if there were tracks of a struggle with a jaguar or any jaguar tracks at all. "With your horse, I could be back in three or four days; but if I walk, they could find and try Poit before I get back."

The old chief thought for a few minutes and then said, "Finding jaguar tracks may not prove anything. With all that blood there, it is quite likely that a cat came to investigate afterward even if it wasn't about to attack."

In the dark, Kyemap's shoulders slumped. Then after a moment he spoke up. "But if there was some sign of a fight, that would prove Poit was telling the truth, wouldn't it?"

"Yes," said the chief softly. "But it doesn't sound like the cat actually attacked. Poit finally gave up on that story, and Mr. Grubb has no scratches. If there was a jaguar, how will you know whether it was there at the time of the shooting or came later to investigate the smell of blood?"

Kyemap considered. "The only thing I can hope for is if I can find a human footprint on top of a jaguar print. That would show that the cat was there first."

"Yes," admitted the chief. "But even if all Poit said was true, finding such a pair of footprints would be as unlikely as finding a stone on the Chaco." (The chief said this because there were almost no stones in the central Chaco. It was one vast plain of silt and sand, washed down from the Andes.) "Nevertheless," said the chief with a sigh, "you may use my horse. It is better to know than not to know. May God go with you!"

Kyemap stood up, mumbling his thank-yous in surprise. Was the old chief coming to believe in Mr. Grubb's God? Sometimes he did attend the Sunday morning services at Waik. His comment certainly was not a Lengua thing to say. The Lengua tradition did not believe in any kind of a good God who would go with, help, or protect anyone. That was definitely a Christian idea.

Chapter 11

On Trial

TWO DAYS LATER, KYEMAP RODE into the village where the helpful native had first brought the wounded Mr. Grubb. Arriving on a healthy horse aroused considerable attention. Everyone wanted to know where he got the horse. Soon the man Kyemap was looking for was standing among the children and other villagers who had gathered around his horse. Directions to where the man had found Grubb were simple enough, but the man had no idea where Grubb had crawled from before he collapsed on the trail.

Kyemap thanked them and headed out of the village with children trailing alongside until they grew tired and turned back. However, the closer Kyemap got to the place where the villager had found Mr. Grubb, the more impossible his task seemed. Finally, he reined in his horse in a small stand of palm trees that looked just like the villager had described. Was it the place? Or would there be another grove farther along? Kyemap went to the edge of the trees. Beyond them the land was flat. As far as he could see, scrub brush extended to the South and swamp to the North. There were no more groves of trees.

He dismounted the horse and began his search. Mr. Grubb had described crossing the river, so he must have come from that direction, from the North, so that is where Kyemap went. There was no trail, but some of the tangles of plants and vines were so thick that no one could have come through them.

At the river, he waded across. Was that how Mr. Grubb had come? How many times had he crossed a river? Had he gone in circles? Grubb had been almost out of his mind with pain and loss of blood. Were any of his memories accurate? On and on, Kyemap trudged through thicker and thicker foliage. Every few feet he waded through swamp water. This was Jaguar Swamp, all right. What if there was a killer jaguar following him even then? Hopefully, the horse that he led behind him would smell it and give him a warning.

He stopped to listen but heard nothing other than frogs and birds. Maybe he ought to give up. How would he ever find the site of the shooting in a tangle like this?

And then, just when he was about to turn around,
he spied a sapling with an arrow wedged between its

limbs. "That's it," he said aloud. Dark, almost black, blood still smeared the arrow shaft and the iron arrowhead. And like Mr. Grubb had said, the tip was bent over. Yanking it out must have hurt more than Kyemap could imagine.

In the soft ground in front of the sapling, Kyemap could see where the missionary had fallen. There was still blood on some of the grass. Carefully, he began tracing Grubb's tracks back to a thicket where the shooting had taken place. Every few feet along the way, there where human footprints—undoubtedly Mr. Grubb's—but no jaguar prints. Finally, Kyemap discovered where Grubb had been hacking on the vines to get through. Grubb's machete was stabbed in the ground where it had probably fallen. Still there were no signs of a great cat.

Kyemap stood up straight and surveyed the area. Poit had claimed to shoot all his arrows at a jaguar. If he had done that, and one had accidentally missed and hit Mr. Grubb in the back, then the jaguar must have been beyond Grubb, and Poit must have been shooting from that direction. Grubb had said Poit was only five or so yards away.

Kyemap tied the horse to a bush and carefully walked to the place he had calculated Poit to be. There, indeed, were prints of Poit's bare feet in the soft ground. He turned around to face where Grubb had been hacking at the thicket with his machete. But the more Kyemap looked at the scene, the more impossible Poit's story seemed. If there had been a great cat in that thicket, how could he have seen it through the dense undergrowth? How could he have hoped to hit it with arrows? How could the cat have been in the process of attacking Mr. Grubb? Nothing could have gotten through that dense tangle, at least not quickly.

One thing was certain, there was no sign of a fight with a wild animal. In fact, there were no tracks of a jaguar anywhere. But how could Kyemap be sure? Maybe he was in the wrong spot. After all, both Grubb and Poit had been struggling to get through the underbrush for some time before the shooting. So even though he had found the machete, maybe the shooting had occurred to one side or the other.

Kyemap was turning aside to check out other options when he noticed something under a bush. He reached for the long tan rods and pulled out four iron-tipped arrows.

Kyemap sighed as though all the air he had ever breathed was leaving his lungs. There was no doubt. His cousin Poit had not shot all five arrows at a jaguar as he had claimed. There had been no jaguar! Poit had shot one arrow at Grubb, intending to kill him.

✧ ✧ ✧ ✧

Two years ago Kyemap would have refused to be alone at night out on the Chaco for fear of wandering evil spirits, but Mr. Grubb had helped him conquer that fear. At this point, the thing he feared most was facing other people when he knew his cousin was guilty of trying to kill Mr. Grubb. On his way back to Paisiam, Kyemap rode around villages and settlements and avoided meeting people on the trail whenever he could. At night he camped alone with nothing but a small fire and his striped blanket. Of course, Chief Mechi's horse tethered nearby was some comfort, but still he felt edgy. He knew that an awful confrontation awaited him somewhere ahead, and it wouldn't be with a ghost.

He would have to face his cousin with the truth of what he had discovered. He would have to tell the elders and other villagers about the proof he had found. That might seal Poit's fate. And if it led to Poit's execution, he might be next.

As he rode along the next day over the dry and dusty trail, Kyemap again went over the whole experience in his mind. Poit had come to Waik to discover whether Mr. Grubb was the one the old Lengua prophecies promised, the one who would reveal the mysteries of the spirit world. It seemed that Poit believed what Mr. Grubb said—at least he worked very hard to become Mr. Grubb's "number one man."

Kyemap straightened himself on the horse's back. Poit had stolen that position from him. Nevertheless, he admitted to himself, that was a small matter when his cousin's life was at stake—and maybe his own, too.

Mr. Grubb had entrusted Poit with a herd of cattle while he went away to England, but Poit had stolen them for himself, probably concluding that

Mr. Grubb was not God's messenger after all. When Mr. Grubb returned, Poit had become afraid that he would get in trouble for killing the cattle. And to cover one sin, he had committed a greater one in trying to kill Mr. Grubb.

The hours passed with the miles as Kyemap reviewed again and again what had happened. Why had Poit become so afraid that he would attempt murder? Yes, he would have been in trouble with Mr. Grubb for having killed the cattle, but that would have only been Mr. Grubb's displeasure. Unlike other foreigners who had entered the Chaco or some of the whites that the Indians met along the Paraguay River or in the town of Concepción, Mr. Grubb had never beaten or hurt anyone. All over the Chaco he was known for being kind and fair. So what had Poit feared so much that he thought he had to kill Mr. Grubb?

Darkness was descending and Kyemap was approaching the village of Paisiam when the answer finally came to him. It was greed that had motivated Poit. He wanted to be the most important Indian on the Chaco. When it looked like being Mr. Grubb's assistant would give him that position, he took that route. When Grubb went away, Poit couldn't imagine him coming back, so he decided to use the cattle to become the most important person in the western Chaco. But when Mr. Grubb returned, both plans fell apart. Mr. Grubb was about to discover the missing cattle and would not trust Poit any longer, and he would take away the rest of the cattle. That's when

Poit must have decided to kill him. With Grubb out of the way by an "accident," at least Poit could continue buying his importance with the remaining cattle.

Poor Poit! Mr. Grubb would say he was trying to be something he was not—foolish ambition. Mr. Grubb was eager to help the Indians become everything they could be, but not based on cheating and falsehoods.

✧ ✧ ✧ ✧

An orange light from the huge bonfire in the center of Paisiam glowed in the sky over the village as Kyemap walked the horse into Chief Mechi's corral. He closed the gate and made sure there was water in the trough. Then he grabbed a handful of straw and rubbed the horse down before removing the simple halter and giving the animal a slap on the rump. The horse kicked up its heels and then trotted around the corral while throwing its head from side to side celebrating its freedom.

Upset by his discovery in the Jaguar Swamp, Kyemap walked slowly into the village, looking between the huts to see the loud gathering around the fire. The closer he got, the more he could hear people yelling in angry voices. Then, startled, he saw Poit, tied to a post with his arms behind him. He was close enough to the bonfire to see the dark tracks where Poit's sweat had run down his dirty face.

They had found Poit and the trial had already begun!

An elder from a neighboring village took a long drink from his gourd of beer and then yelled in Poit's face so that a spray of beer accompanied his words. "You murdered him, didn't you?"

"No! No!" protested Poit shaking his head vigorously. "I shot my arrows at a jaguar. I was trying to protect Mr. Grubb. I shot all five arrows. If one missed and happened to strike Mr. Grubb, it was an accident. You've got to believe me!"

Another Indian demanded to know why the cowardly Poit left the missionary if it was only an accident. Poit repeated his story that the wounded jaguar was too dangerous and Mr. Grubb was beyond help.

"But he wasn't beyond help! He lived, didn't he?" accused the man.

"How could I know that?" cried Poit desperately.

Kyemap almost stepped forward to contradict Poit with what he had discovered. But he hesitated. He, too, was in danger if Poit was condemned. Maybe they would not need his evidence. After all, his evidence only proved what everyone suspected.

"Even if I did plan to kill him," Poit said defensively, "he didn't die. So you can't condemn me for murder. No one has been killed!" He said it defiantly, like he had finally discovered a way to beat his accusers at their own game.

But the man closest to him spat in Poit's face. "How do we know that Mr. Grubb lives? Many say another spirit lives in his body."

One of the elders shook his finger toward Poit. "If . . . if he is alive, it is no thanks to you," he said through gritted teeth. "Under Lengua law the intent to kill is as serious as the act. You must die!"

Howling in desperation, Poit cried, "The Lengua people have never executed one of their own people for killing a foreigner. You cannot condemn me!"

The same elder took up the challenge. "But Mr. Grubb has become one of us. He is no longer a foreigner. The full Lengua law will be applied to you . . . to you and *all your kin!*" shouted the angry man.

At that, Kyemap panicked and ran back between the huts and out to the corral. He threw open the gate and ran in after the chief's horse. Moments later he was galloping down the moonlit trail toward Waik. There was only one hope remaining.

Chapter 12

A Plea for Mercy

KYEMAP SLIPPED OFF THE SWEATING HORSE to the bare, hard-packed ground of the mission station and walked through moon shadows under the trees to Mr. Grubb's house. The first step creaked in protest as he mounted the porch. Would it awaken Mr. Grubb? Would he come out with his gun to scare away the "ghosts"? Kyemap grinned as he recalled the encounter with old Pinse-Tawa. Hostile witch doctors seemed as pale as the moonlight compared to the blaze of danger that now danced before Poit . . . and Kyemap, too.

He stepped carefully across the porch, through the quiet house, and out back. At one end of the screened-in sleeping porch stood a tent of mosquito netting that glowed dimly orange from the low-burning oil lamp within. Kyemap could see through the hazy netting the form of a man tossing and moaning on the bed. As he approached, he caught a pungent whiff of medicine and noticed beads of sweat glistening on Grubb's sickly-looking forehead.

"Mr. Grubb?" Kyemap said quietly.

Grubb sat up with a start, panting as though he had been having a bad dream, but it was not a dream. The man was sick—sick with a fever that caused him to sway and half close his eyes. "Who's there?" he mumbled, seeing the shadow of Kyemap through the mosquito netting. "What time is it? Is it time to get up? I don't think I can make it today." Then his strength drained away like water from a broken jar, and he melted back onto his pillow with a faint, high-pitched sigh.

Kyemap stepped forward and parted the netting. "Are you all right? Should I get someone?"

Grubb opened his eyes again and stared at Kyemap, slowly bringing him into focus. "Oh, it's you, Kyemap. No, no, don't bother anyone else. Just get me a glass of water, please."

Kyemap sat on the edge of the bed and poured water from a small pitcher on the side table. With a shaky hand the missionary took a sip from the glass and said, "I'll be all right in a day or so. This fever comes and goes." Then he added with a wry grin, "But I always seem to recover." He was quiet for a moment then looked up at Kyemap. "Where have you been the last few days? I haven't seen you around."

Kyemap straightened up. How could he ask a sick man to help him save Poit? Grubb couldn't even get out of bed, let alone travel to Paisiam.

Grubb must have seen the hesitation in his face, because he said, "What's the matter? Has there been more trouble with the witch doctors?"

"No," said Kyemap. And then after a long moment, "It's Poit. They've caught him, and I think they're going to execute him."

Grubb pushed himself up on his pillows. "What's happened?" he said. "What do you know." Kyemap found himself pouring out the whole story, including his trip to the site of the attack and the proof of Poit's guilt that he found there.

Grubb shook his head. "I don't want Poit to die," he said. "Executing him would not solve anything. You must ride back to Paisiam immediately and tell them that I am not dead, and I will be greatly grieved if they execute him. Tell them that is my wish."

When Kyemap hesitated, Grubb said, "Go on, now. You can do it." Then after studying Kyemap's face, he said, "Don't worry about me. I'll be okay. Hunt will look in on me in the morning. Now go." He paused and stared hard into Kyemap's eyes. "What is it? There's something else you haven't told me, isn't there?"

Kyemap took a long breath. "It is the Lengua custom to not let anyone close to a condemned person live so that there won't be any retaliation. I . . . I fear for my life."

"But surely that doesn't include you. You are a distant cousin," said Mr. Grubb.

Kyemap shrugged. "I don't know. The last thing I heard one of the elders say to Poit was, 'The full Lengua law will be applied to you . . . to you and *all your kin!*' I'm afraid that might include me because Poit has been seen with me so often this last year."

Mr. Grubb shook his head. "Some of these customs have got to change," he said. "Look, I don't want anyone to die on my account—not you, not any of Poit's other relatives, not even Poit himself. You've got to go tell them that! Convince them that there is to be no more killing." He watched Kyemap's face for a few moments and then added, "Remember how God protected you that night under the bottle trunk tree? Remember how He gave you courage when you prayed to Him? That's what you've got to do now. You go and pray on the way, and I'll stay here and pray. Now, be off with you."

❖ ❖ ❖ ❖

It was nearly noon when Kyemap got back to Paisiam. A foul-smelling smoke hung over the whole village and stung his eyes. Kyemap did not see Poit anywhere, but he soon found Chief Mechi and several elders from other villages sleeping under their blankets in the shade of three palm trees.

Kyemap ground-tied the horse and approached

the sleepers. Given the amount of beer they had been drinking the night before, they would probably have pounding headaches and not want to be awakened. In fact, it might be difficult to awaken them. Still, his assignment was urgent, and finally he gently shook the chief's shoulder.

Surprisingly, Chief Mechi sat straight up as though he hadn't been asleep at all. "What do you want?" he said in a clear and firm voice. It was loud enough that some of the other men stirred.

"I-I've returned your horse," Kyemap said tentatively.

"Is that a reason to wake me up?" said the chief with a scowl. "Just put it in the corral, and get out of here before . . ." He looked around with his marbled eyes that saw so poorly as though realizing for the first time how loudly he was talking. He lowered his voice. ". . . before some of these men wake up and find you here."

"But I need to talk to you," said Kyemap in hushed tones. "Poit must not be executed!"

The chief stood up then, and his blanket slid off his shoulder onto another man. That man woke up, and before Kyemap realized what was happening, all the other men were sitting up, rubbing their eyes at him.

"Who's this?" said one of the elders. "Has the killer's cousin come to surrender himself?"

Two of the other elders stood up quickly, at first holding their heads and swaying dizzily. Then they stumbled forward and grabbed Kyemap's arms. "We have him now," said one of the men.

"Wait," said the chief, putting up a hand. "Did you find some proof of your cousin's innocence?" he asked Kyemap.

Kyemap avoided the question and quickly said, "I come from Mr. Grubb. He sends a plea for mercy for Poit. He does not want you to execute him."

"But what did you find on your trip?" pressed the chief. "You did go to the West as you asked, didn't you?"

"Yes, but—"

"Well?" urged the chief. "Did you find the place of the attack?"

Kyemap nodded, then said yes, realizing that the chief would have trouble seeing just his head nod.

"Don't be difficult, boy," said the chief. "What did you learn?"

So Kyemap told about what he had found, ending with, "But I've also talked to Mr. Grubb and told him what I found. He wants to forgive Kyemap."

"Sounds like you are looking out for yourself," muttered the elder who held Kyemap's right arm.

Again the chief held up his hand. "If what you found proves that Poit tried to kill Grubb, why should we not have executed him?"

"Because . . . because—" Suddenly, Kyemap realized that the chief had used the past tense. Had they already put Poit to death? "Because he . . . because Grubb doesn't want *any* killing, none at all!" Though his words were firm, his voice trailed off as he saw in the eyes of the men that the deed had already been done. "Is he already dead?" he asked the chief.

"At first light this morning," said the chief gravely. "But since your findings prove him guilty, then we did right. Besides, he made a full confession." The chief shrugged as though executing Poit was all they could have done under those circumstances. "At first Poit had wanted to use the gun, but there were no bullets. He decided to lead Grubb into Jaguar Swamp. But no cat came, so he shot Grubb thinking that wild animals would quickly devour his body before anyone found it. He was wrong," the chief added matter-of-factly.

"But Mr. Grubb didn't want *anyone* killed for this. He *forgives* Poit," said Kyemap.

"The boy's just trying to save his own skin," said one of the elders.

"That's right," said another. "Whoever heard of forgiving such an evil person?"

"Especially forgiving the person who tried to kill you!"

"God did," said Kyemap, surprising himself. But as he looked around at the Lengua elders, the Gospel that Mr. Grubb had been teaching him began to make sense. "God forgives us all. All of us are evil sometimes. We lie. We grab the best things for ourselves. We are mean to other people. We all do it. God calls that sin, but He forgives us if we will forgive one another." Suddenly, he realized that he was preaching to them like Mr. Grubb did on Sunday mornings.

Surprised by this Good News that most of them

had never heard, the elders listened as Kyemap explained how God loved humans so much that He sent His only Son to save them, even though people were so sinful that they killed Jesus.

"If the people killed God's Son," asked one of the men, "how can He forgive us?"

"Because God raised Him from the dead," said Kyemap. "Many people saw Him." Shaking his head earnestly, he said, "This was no ghost. Jesus was really alive again. Many people talked to Him and touched Him . . . and ate with Him," he added, remembering the proof he had discovered that a paca and not a ghost had visited him that night at the bottle trunk tree.

Chief Mechi nodded his head soberly and said to Kyemap, "We must talk. Take my horse to the corral. When you return, we will have made our decision."

With wide eyes, Kyemap looked around at the other men. Decision? What decision were they going to make? Had they really intended to kill him right then? He backed away, stumbling over a stick and almost falling. He recovered, turned, and ran to the horse.

As he walked it back toward the corral, Kyemap slowed, scuffing his toes in the dust. Was he a fake? Had he only been preaching the Gospel to the elders in hopes that they wouldn't kill him? Of course he wanted them to accept it and not kill him, but he hadn't accepted it himself. Oh, he recognized that the things he had been saying were true, but he hadn't done anything about them. He hadn't ac-

cepted God's forgiveness for himself. He hadn't decided to give his whole life to God in gratitude for
forgiving him. He hadn't asked Jesus to live in his
heart. Those were all things Mr. Grubb had said
were part of really *believing*, part of becoming a true
Christian.

So why had he been preaching to the elders? Was
it just to save his own life?

"O God," he prayed quietly, "please forgive me
and make my life new. I am sorry for using your
Gospel just to save my own life. I want to become a

Christian now, no matter what happens. And if my life is spared, I will go straight to Mr. Grubb and tell him that I am ready to be baptized so everyone will know that I am a Christian."

For some reason, Kyemap realized his fear was gone. With new courage he returned to Chief Mechi and faced the elders.

"We cannot do anything about Poit," the chief announced with great solemnity. "He has already been executed. But we have decided to honor the rest of Mr. Grubb's request, and we will not kill any of his relatives. You are free to go."

✧ ✧ ✧ ✧

A short time later, Kyemap became the first baptized convert among the Lengua people. With the baptismal waters streaming down his face, he said, "From now on, I would like to be called by the name of Philip, because, like Philip in the Bible, I want to become an evangelist and tell people the *Tasik Amyaa,* the Good News."

And he did.

More About Barbrooke Grubb

BARBROOKE GRUBB WAS BORN on August 11, 1865, at Liberton in Midlothian, Scotland. As a boy he delighted in wrestling and feats of strength and was filled with mischief. He completed his education at George Watson College in Edinburgh, Scotland, where his interest in geography and ancient history led to his study of the habits of primitive peoples. He also took a medical course in which he and a friend both cut themselves accidentally in the dissecting room. His friend died within forty-eight hours, and Grubb remained sick for nearly a year.

In 1884 he met Dwight Moody and Ira Sankey, the dynamic evangelists from the United States, and ended up devoting his life to missions. On his nineteenth birthday, Grubb decided to join the South

American Missionary Society and two years later went to the Falkland Islands, where he spent four years. But he always felt called to the Indian tribes of the northern interior.

Nothing pleased him more than his assignment in 1890 to the unexplored interior of Paraguay, known as the Chaco, and the wild tribes of Indians who lived there.

Initially, Grubb employed the unusual (at that time) tactic of going right into the interior, first to explore the territory and make friends, and then to live right with the Indians rather than build a large station on the perimeter of the field to which the Indians came. Though later he did set up mission stations such as Waikthlatingmangyalwa, they were in the heart of the Chaco and were designed for the sake of the Indians rather than the convenience and comfort of the missionaries. At these stations, the Indians learned better agricultural techniques, industry, and the Gospel. Even at the mission stations, Grubb's unusual acceptance by the Indians was based on his willingness to live among them in an unthreatening manner.

Grubb was not very good at foreign languages. Lengua was the only language of the Chaco that he spoke easily, and in that he broke almost all the grammatical rules. But he had a gift for picking up enough essential words and phrases in half a dozen languages to make himself understood. He communicated more by speaking from the heart than as a skilled linguist.

Grubb's fearlessness and Christian love so won the confidence of the Indians that the government of Paraguay appointed him commissioner for the Chaco.

On May 15, 1901, Grubb married Mary Bridges in Buenos Aires. She, of course, joined him in the Chaco, but Grubb never had the assistance of more than four other European missionaries in his work.

Some of his greatest challenges came from the oppressive superstitions of the people promoted by witch doctors who kept the people in bondage while living off their fears. Though Grubb was deliberately contemptuous of the witch doctors (so as to break their cruel power over the people), he nevertheless studied their mysteries and learned secrets otherwise hidden from all those outside their guild. Politically incorrect as it now may sound, he concluded that ridicule was the safest weapon to reduce a witch doctor's power among his own people.

Even though the number of baptized believers in the Lengua church did not grow beyond two hundred during his ministry among them, the general life for the majority of the people was profoundly transformed. Tribal wars ceased, infanticide ended, hunger (from a nomadic lifestyle and failure to plant crops and prepare for the future) was overcome, and the general health of the people was greatly improved. With the help of his assistants, Grubb also translated hymns, prayers, and most of the New Testament into Lengua.

One of his greatest concerns while working among the Indians was that the government had already divided up the Chaco into county-sized lots to sell to land speculators intent on making their own fortunes. Neither the sellers nor the potential buyers had set foot in this wilderness, but they were ready to grab it out from under the Indians for whom it had been home for countless generations. Using his own savings and all the funds he could raise elsewhere, Grubb set about to prevent this theft by purchasing the land in the name of the Indians. It was his vision that the Lengua people would become a self-supporting, self-governing community. His goal was for each family to possess its own livestock and homestead, equipped to engage in agriculture or in the arts and crafts such as woodworking, pottery, weaving, or sewing.

The mission to the Lenguas, which was started in 1890, was fully established by 1910 when Grubb had already begun work with the Toothli and Suhin tribes of the West and the Sanapana in the North. Grubb then moved to northern Argentina and Bolivia, where he established a strong mission among the Matacos of the Bermejo and a prosperous beginning among the people of the Pilcomayo. He also began tentative efforts among the Tobas and converted many among the Tapui Indians of Bolivia. It is no wonder that in his lifetime he became known around the world as the "Livingstone of South America."

Grubb accomplished all this before he died on May 28, 1930.

For Further Reading

Davidson, Norman J. *Barbrooke Grubb: Pathfinder*. London: Seeley, Service & Co., Ltd., 1924.

Grubb, W. Barbrooke. *A Church in the Wilds*. London: Seeley, Service & Co., Ltd., 1914.

Grubb, W. Barbrooke. *An Unknown People in an Unknown Land*. London: Seeley, Service & Co., Ltd., 1914.

Hunt, Richard James. *The Livingstone of South America*. Philadelphia: J. B. Lippincott, 1933.

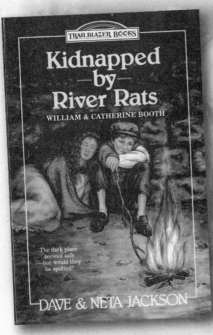

"I love the TRAILBLAZER BOOKS. I can't wait to read them all!"

— Josiah, ND

Have *you* read them all? Here is a sneak peek at another TRAILBLAZER BOOK you don't want to miss!

The Bandit of Ashley Downs

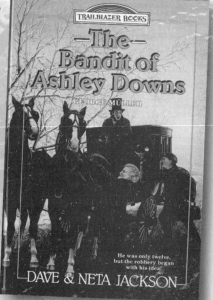

Twelve-year-old Curly is an orphan, acrobat, and master pickpocket. When he overhears that a church is raising money for an orphan house, he plans an armed robbery that promises to bring him enough money for a lifetime.

But is Curly in for more trouble than he bargained for? If he is caught, which fate would be scarier—to be sent to prison, or to the very orphanage from which he stole the money? Would George Müller, the man in charge of the orphanage, make Curly into a slave to earn back at least a portion of the money? Or might they do something even worse?

Curly is in for the biggest surprise of his young life!

For a complete listing of TRAILBLAZER BOOKS, see page 2!

◆ ◆

Available now for $5.99 each from your local Christian bookstore or from Bethany House Publishers. Mail orders, please add $3.00.

The Leader in Christian Fiction!

BETHANY HOUSE PUBLISHERS

11400 Hampshire Avenue South
Minneapolis, Minnesota 55438

www.bethanyhouse.com